"I am not a little girl anymore," she said huskily.

"No, but you are still very much a little fool."

"Is this so foolish?" she asked, snuggling closer. His efforts to thrust her away were of no avail. But he was no longer trying very hard. Her head bent lower, her golden hair cascading over him, brushing against his cheek as she dared to steal a kiss from the taut line of his mouth. It was barely a whisper, shy and tremulous enough to break what remained of Max's self-control.

Instead of pushing her away, he crushed her hard against him, taking possession of her lips with a ruthless fervor. He caught one hand in the silky tangle of curls at the nape of her neck. Holding her captive, his mouth greedily devoured hers. . . .

MISTRESS MISCHIEF

Susan Carroll

FAWCETT CREST • NEW YORK

A Fawcett Crest Book
Published by Ballantine Books
Copyright © 1992 by Susan Coppula

All rights reserved under International and Pan-American Copyright Conventions. Published in the United States by Ballantine Books, a division of Random House, Inc., New York, and simultaneously in Canada by Random House of Canada Limited, Toronto.

Library of Congress Catalog Card Number: 92-90157

ISBN 0-449-21694-2

Manufactured in the United States of America

First Edition: September 1992

Chapter 1

Leon Auguste Barry, the Viscount Raincliffe, was not yet cold in his grave. His lordship had been laid to rest among the family tombs upon a Sunday afternoon. By the following morning, his eldest son and heir, Sir Wilfred Barry, prepared triumphantly to evict his stepmama from Dunhaven Manor.

For two long years, Sir Wilfred, his thin, sharp features twitching with disapproval, had endured the presence of *that woman* polluting the halls of his ancestral home, that yellow-haired strumpet, that fortune-hunting minx who had so beguiled his father, making a complete fool of the old viscount.

But when the will had been read out after the funeral services, it appeared that the late Lord Raincliffe had finally come to his senses. Not a single mention had been made of his second wife, not so much as a pound note left to her. Sir Wilfred, who had lived in expectation of seeing over half his inheritance bequeathed to the scheming wench, had been hard put not to burst forth with an unseemly "huzzah."

The new Lord Raincliffe had wasted little time in informing his stepmama that her presence at Dunhaven was no longer welcome. Now, as he paced the great hall, consulting his pocket watch, he impatiently awaited her departure.

The manor was draped with black crepe in memory of its late master, and the atmosphere at Dunhaven was unusually somber now as Frederica Eleanor Barry, the Dowager Countess of Raincliffe, emerged from her bedchamber.

Struggling with the weight of her portmanteau, she closed the door. The youngest footman, John, would have darted forward to her aid if he had dared, because for a wicked adventuress, Lady Raincliffe possessed a remarkably sweet countenance. Her delicate, heart-shaped face was framed by a halo of golden ringlets. Her complexion cream and roses, she might have looked all softness and innocence but for the strength to be found in her stubborn chin and the naughty sparkle to be discovered in her deep blue eyes.

But her expression this morning was subdued, far more so than her apparel. With her diminutive frame garbed in a pelisse of bright apple green, her straw bonnet trimmed with artificial cherries and tied with a coquelicot ribbon, no one had ever appeared less like a grieving widow. Any sorrow she felt had to be detected beneath the lush sweep of her gold-tipped lashes, and that was no easy task. At the age of twenty, Freddie was already a most accomplished actress, having learned a long time before how to guard her more tender emotions from the scorn of the world.

Switching the heavy portmanteau to her other hand, she mustered all her dignity and set forth down the long gallery that connected the east wing with the main part of the house. Gray morning light filtered through the tall, latticed windows, revealing the vast chamber to be a hive of bustling footmen. Most of them averted their gaze as Freddie passed by, refusing to meet her eyes.

Trust servants to always know when one was no longer a person of any account, she thought dryly. She watched as the men busied themselves, carting away some of her late husband's prized possessions, the heavily carved Jacobean chairs that like a pair of thrones had flanked the fireplace, the brass-plated torchère, the quaint old fire screen.

Sir Wilfred was apparently wasting little time in making his ownership felt, altering Dunhaven to suit his own mundane tastes. Freddie noted with some amusement that her portrait was already gone, leaving a rectangular shadow in the empty space along the dark oak wainscoting. Doubtless her stepson had burned the painting. Not that she much cared, having thought that the likeness had made her look wretchedly fubsy-faced.

She was far more disturbed to see that the footmen were removing the portrait of Leon as well, likely to consign it to one of the rooms at the far back of the house with the rest of the unwanted furnishings.

Painted upon the occasion of their marriage, it was a full-length pose of the late viscount, ever the gallant in his satin knee breeches, his frock coat frothing with lace at the cuffs, his white powdered wig pulled back into a neat queue reminiscent of another era. But Leon had never apologized for his old-fashioned attire.

As he had once told her, "Not even for you, babe, will I make a cake of m'self, aping the fashions of these young sparks, tricked out in yaller breeches, m'hair cut to resemble some dead Roman."

And although Freddie had often teased him about it, she had quite agreed with him. Leon had been magnificent in his powder and patch, always the grand seigneur. The French artist had captured that regal bearing. Monsieur Le Brun had done nothing to soften or flatter Leon's advancing years, but there had been no necessity. Despite the lines that time and the devil had carved in Leon's aquiline features, the roguish light in his eyes had been unquenchable.

A faint sigh escaped Freddie. She would have gone down on both knees and begged Wilfred to let her have the painting if she thought that would have done any good. As it was, all she could do was watch the footmen cart it off to gather dust.

She turned away, slowly recommencing her final journey through the manor that had been her home for the past two years, the one place in her misbegotten life where she had almost been happy. But Freddie refused to allow herself any sentimental memories about Dunhaven. After all, it had been a man she had loved, not a place. And he was gone.

When she reached the top of the grand staircase, she glanced down to the marble-tiled hall below. At the foot of the stairs stood her stepson, some fifteen years Freddie's senior, a stick of a man with pinched nostrils and small, close-set eyes. Behind him stood his two unmarried sisters equally scrawny and self-righteous. To his left hovered his meek wife, Harriet, nervously wringing her mittened hands.

Sir Wilfred had not as yet deigned to bring any of his children to Dunhaven. Doubtless to the last, he feared having his offspring contaminated by Freddie's presence. The supposition did not pain Freddie. Assuming Sir Wilfred's heirs to be molded in his own image, she had never desired to make their acquaintance. Indeed, at the moment she rather wished she had never been introduced to the rest of the family.

The elder generation of Barrys were all attired in unrelenting black, reminding Freddie of a flock of beady-eyed crows come to pick over her bones. She might have been daunted to face such a disapproving throng, except that she could hear the echoes of her late husband's voice in her ear, Leon lamenting in that droll way of his: *Stap me, m'dear. Just look at 'em. How did an old rip like me ever come to father such a sanctimonious bunch of prigs? I would suspect I had been made a cuckold, but m'first wife was so stuffed with virtue, I don't even have the comfort of that notion.*

Despite the grimness of Freddie's situation, the memory caused her lips to quiver. She sauntered down the broad stairs, achieving a deal of grace despite the awkwardness of balancing the valise. Wilfred's gaze raked her up and down, regarding the bright folds of her pelisse with a thunderstruck expression.

"Madam!" he said. "Fie upon you. You could at least have had the decency to put on the semblance of mourning for my father."

Setting down the portmanteau that was causing her arm to ache, Freddie smiled sweetly. "I saw no occasion for it. You and your sisters seem to be doing more than an adequate job of that. Besides, milord never liked me to wear black."

And the whisper of Leon's voice came to her again, some of his final instructions to her as he had lain dying.

And don't you dare be decking yourself out like a magpie lest you want me coming back from my grave to haunt you. You be sure to wear that bonnet I like, the one with the saucy ribbons. It will give me something pleasant to think on when I am down trading quips in hell.

The memory this time of that familiar, raspy

voice became a little too poignant, and Freddie felt
a thickness gather in her throat. She swallowed
hard, determined not to think of Leon again until
she was clear of this house. She would perish herself before she gave these smug fools the satisfaction of seeing her weep.

She noted Wilfred moistening his lips, his thin
chest filling with air, and realized that he could not
let the occasion pass without delivering one last diatribe against her.

"Madam—"

Freddie cut him off with an airy wave of her
hand. "Oh, pray, my . . ." No, she could not do it.
She could not accord him the dignity of Leon's title.

"Sir Wilfred," she continued, "let us part for once
without quarreling. I trust you have had the carriage brought round."

"You trust wrong, madam," he sneered. "It is
but a short walk to the crossroads. If you hurry, you
may contrive to catch the afternoon stage."

Like a Delphic chorus, his sisters murmured
their satisfied agreement while Freddie was momentarily shaken. Curse him! The crossroads was
nearly ten miles away and the skies already threatening rain. Freddie would not have thought that
even Wilfred could be such a toad as that, but she
managed to conceal her dismay. Not so his wife
Harriet, who paled and faltered, "Oh, n-no, my lord.
Surely we could at least offer Frederica the use of
the old brougham—"

"No, we could not," Wilfred snapped. "Let this
strumpet leave as she came, sneaking through the
gates."

"Actually," Freddie said, "I arrived in a coach
and four with gilt-trimmed wheels and peacock blue
cushions. Six outriders and two postilions. But I
know what pain such an outlay of money would oc-

casion you, my dear Wilfred, and I would not want to leave you suffering from an attack of biliousness."

Sir Wilfred's face washed a dull red. In a spirit of pure mischief, Freddie could not resist adding, "So I suppose that nothing remains but for you to come kiss your mama good-bye."

Wilfred looked as though he would strangle on his own neck cloth. He became nearly incoherent as he spluttered, "I'd—I'd sooner box your ears."

"Would you?" Freddie inquired amicably. "I confess, I would think the better of you if you did. But you have always been naught but a bully, all bluster."

It was a melancholy prospect, to think of this mean-spirited scarecrow of a man stepping into Leon's shoes. But Freddie refused to dwell on what she could not remedy. Gathering up the burden of her baggage once more, she swept past her affronted stepson.

She paused to press Harriet's hand and murmur loud enough for Wilfred to hear, "Take heart, my dear. With such spleen, he's bound to be taken off with a fit of apoplexy someday. That, at least, will give you something to look forward to."

Harriet gave a shocked gasp, and Sir Wilfred thundered out, "Why—you—you wretched woman. 'Tis you who will come to a bad end one day."

"So I have been told since I was eight years old," Freddie said. "It is hardly a novel prediction, Sir Wilfred."

"Be gone, you Jezebel!" He swept one finger, pointing toward the front door.

But the melodramatic gesture was entirely wasted, for Freddie was already heading in that direction. Chawton, the old butler, stepped forward to open the door for her, his gaze fixed rigidly ahead.

Freddie thought his eyes looked slightly reddened. It was not surprising that even this stiff-necked manservant should have been weeping for his late master. What did astonish her was the low whisper that followed her out the door.

"God keep you, milady."

Startled, Freddie half looked back, but the door was already being closed in her face. It was far easier to pretend that she had never heard the words. Insults and disapproval she knew how to deal with. Any show of kindness always proved her undoing.

Turning her back on Dunhaven, she stepped out from the shelter of the portico onto the gravel drive leading away from the house, cheerfully consigning Sir Wilfred and all his kind to the devil.

But beneath her spirit of bravado came the first flutterings of panic as a gust of October wind penetrated the unlined silk of her pelisse, the muslin gown she wore beneath. Shivering, she stared down the lane that wound past Dunhaven's broad lawns, the stately line of sycamore trees showing their first hintings of autumn gold. The drive looked bleak and empty, a road leading to nowhere.

For one deemed such a hardened fortune hunter, she had little to show for being the widow of one of the wealthiest peers in England, only a small cache of jewels and what little she had managed to save out of her pin money. She had no notion of where she was going or even how to get there.

"What am I going to do, Leon?" she murmured, racking her brain for some of the worldly wisdom Leon had dispensed to her so freely over the brief course of their marriage.

On one of those rare occasions when he could be induced to be serious, she recollected, he had said to her with a melancholy sigh, "Ah, the time has ever been out of joint for us, my dear. If only you had been born forty years sooner or I much later. But there is little sense repining over that. I have been selfish enough to rob you of a brief portion of your youth. But when I am gone—"

She had tried to hush him, ever hating to hear him talk of his dying or even to think of it. But he had insisted, continuing on to say, "When I am gone, don't bury yourself in the country. Life was not meant to be such a dull affair. Find yourself some gaiety, some laughter, some adventure. London is the best place for that. And then find yourself some handsome young buck who will make you a proper husband."

Freddie frowned at the memory. It had always troubled Leon that he had been no longer capable of being what he had deemed a "proper" husband to her. Any visits to her bed at night had been only to tuck her in, to plant a chaste kiss upon her brow. Not fully understanding the allure of the physical aspect of marriage, Freddie had not found anything lacking in Leon's behavior. But she comprehended enough to realize it had been a source of deep humiliation to him and she had vowed even after his death to keep his secret forever.

Missing Leon, grieving for him as she did, the prospect of finding "some handsome young buck" held no appeal for her. But she was still young enough to long for the gaiety and adventure that Leon had spoken of.

London is the best place, Leon had said. And so to London she would go.

Valiantly squaring her shoulders, Freddie started down the drive. Setting out on an adventure might have been a great deal more appealing if one didn't have to carry one's own bag, or if the lane ahead was not so infernally long. But she was not about to waste time complaining.

When she finally saw the park gates and the lodgekeeper's house looming up ahead of her, she heaved a sigh of relief, trying to forget she had yet another eight miles to go before she reached the crossroads. At least it was not raining yet.

But her relief faded when she observed a tall figure garbed in a drab brown cloak step away from the shelter of the lodge's whitewashed stone walls. Freddie's heart sank. No, it could not be. But it was. There was only one woman in all of Somerset, perhaps all of England, with a pair of shoulders so broad, she could have been a prizefighter— Miss Theodora Applegate, Leon's niece by marriage, a poor relation of his first wife.

As Freddie approached, the middle-aged spinster regarded her through reproachful dark eyes, the breeze tossing strands of her lank brown hair free of her prim bonnet. Her mournful expression served only to accent the leanness of Theodora's features, her long chin, her even longer nose. As Leon had been wont to remark, "Dora would have been a handsome filly if only she had been a horse."

Freddie cringed, damning herself for a coward, but she had tried to avoid taking leave of Dora. The woman was the one person at Dunhaven besides Leon who was sincerely attached to Freddie. There was nothing Freddie hated so much as tearful good-byes, and she had hoped the letter she had slipped beneath Dora's pillow last night would have spared her this one. But it seemed she was not to escape so lightly.

As she came to a halt in front of Miss Applegate, Freddie did not give her a chance to speak, but immediately began to scold. "Dora, what are you doing here? Did I not beg you in my note to spare us both a parting that can only be painful?"

"And so I am." Dora shuffled her feet, looking

sheepish, but there was a most dogged light in her eyes all the same. "There won't be any parting. I am coming with you."

"What!" For the first time, Freddie noted that beneath the cloak peeked the hem of Dora's best traveling gown and stacked behind her was a neat pile of bandboxes.

"My dear Dora," Freddie said. "Of course you are doing no such thing."

"You don't want me?" Dora faltered.

"It isn't that at all. But where I am going . . . 'tis just not possible to take you with me."

"Oh." Dora's shoulders slumped. "You are going back to your uncle's house, then."

"Good Lord, no!" Freddie shuddered at the mere thought of the cheerless, unloving home in which she had spent her childhood. "That is the last place where I would go even if my aunt and uncle would have me back. No, I am entirely on my own now, with scarcely a feather to fly with."

"I know. I heard the terms of that infamous will." Dora's stolid features darkened with a rare flash of anger. "I cannot believe that Uncle Leon would have treated you so shabbily."

"It was not his fault, but mine. He spoke of changing the will many times, but I always diverted him. There were so many more pleasant things for us to do than closet ourselves with a bunch of musty solicitors." Freddie's lips curved into a wry smile at what had been perhaps her greatest folly, but she still could not bring herself to regret it. Leon had had Wilfred to flap about him like a great black buzzard, reminding his father of death. Freddie had only ever wanted him to think about living.

Even at the end, when Leon had begged for the attorney to be fetched, Freddie's main concern had been sending for the doctor. By the time the solicitor had arrived, it had already been far too late.

Dora gave an indignant sniff. "Wilfred should have done something. He must know his papa always meant to have provided for you. If my cousin has a generous bone in his body—"

"If he has, he broke it a long time ago," Freddie interrupted. "But you see how it is with me, Dora. I would gladly take you with me, but I have no home to offer you. I must live now entirely by my own wits."

"Then that is why you need me," Dora persisted. "I will be your companion, lend you an air of respectability."

"I don't intend to be respectable anymore," Freddie said recklessly. "For once, I may try to be just as bad and wicked as everyone has always thought me."

"Oh!" Dora appeared momentarily daunted, then said stoutly, "Well . . . well, good! That shall suit me. I have always wanted to be a wicked woman myself."

When Freddie broke into a reluctant laugh, Dora added fiercely, "Truly!"

"My dearest friend," Freddie murmured. Touched more than she cared to admit by the woman's loyalty, she gently tucked back some of the straying tendrils beneath the rim of Dora's bonnet. "You cannot know what you are saying. Your home has always been here at Dunhaven, your family . . ."

Dora's large brown eyes filled with tears. "You are my family, the only one who truly ever cared for me."

Freddie wanted to assure her that was not true, but found she could not. Even Leon had sometimes been less than kind to poor Dora, introducing her in that teasing way of his as "m'inheritance from my late wife, along with the silverplate and some odd bits of china."

"I am sure Sir Wilfred will insist you continue on here at Dunhaven. You are his cousin," Freddie said lamely.

"Oh, aye. Wilfred has already told me that he understands his obligation toward me." Dora's tears brimmed over, trickling down her sallow cheeks. "He hopes that I will be properly grateful and continue to make myself useful. *You* more than anyone should understand what that means, what it feels like to be an unwanted poor relation."

Freddie winced, struck to the heart by Dora's words more than her tears. Because she did understand, only too well. Freddie had only to close her eyes to summon up her aunt Jameson's cold voice, speaking as though Freddie were not even present.

"Oh, yes, the child is a sad trial to us, wild to a fault. My late brother's daughter, you know, left on our hands when she was only eight. Quite a financial burden considering we have four girls of our own. One would not mind so much if Frederica would contrive to be more obliging. But still, one must do one's duty."

God preserve her forever, Freddie thought bitterly, from people who did their duty. And preserve Dora, too.

Digging out her lace-edged handkerchief, Freddie mopped at the woman's tears. "There now, please don't cry anymore, Dora. You know I cannot bear waterworks." And though she thought herself quite mad, she heard herself adding, "If you truly wish it, you may come with me."

Dora blew her nose gustily into Freddie's linen. "Oh, F-Freddie, do you mean it?"

Freddie could do no more than nod her head before she was enveloped in a huge bear hug. Dora lit up with a beaming smile that rendered her face quite appealing. Spinning on her heel, she called out to the bushes at the side of the lodge.

"Everything is all right. Her ladyship says we can go with her."

"We?" Freddie repeated faintly. Before she could question Dora or even protest, two more figures popped out from behind the shrubberies, an elderly man with rheumy eyes and age spots on his balding pate, accompanied by a pert girl with round apple cheeks and flyaway curls. Freddie had no difficulty in recognizing Dunhaven's old coachman and the upper-story housemaid, but she shifted uneasily.

"Dora, whatever is going on here?"

"It's that horrid Wilfred," Dora said, dragging the bashful coachman forward. "Can you believe it? He has already pensioned off poor Stubbins."

Freddie had no difficulty believing it. Mr. Stubbins was half blind, and some of the more recent outings she had taken with him at the reins had left Freddie thinking she should have paid more heed to making out *her* will. It had been inevitable that the old man would have to give up his position.

"That is too bad, Stubbins," Freddie said, "but surely you will be glad to retire to a cozy cottage."

"Not on the miserly pension Sir Wilfred has given him," Dora said. "Such a paltry sum would not keep a beggar alive."

Freddie's gaze turned from the wistful old man to the housemaid. "And Till?" she asked with a sinking heart. "Never tell me she has also been dismissed."

Dora nodded vigorously. "Turned off without a character because . . ." As she leaned forward to whisper in Freddie's ear, Till cast down her eyes, blushing bright red.

"Oh!" Freddie said, unable to keep her gaze from drifting to the girl's thickening middle.

"But everything will be fine now," Dora said. "I knew with your kind heart you would never turn them away. And we will need servants in our new household."

Freddie rolled her eyes. Dora did not seem to comprehend they might consider themselves fortunate if they managed to have a house, let alone a household. She tried to find a polite but firm way to explain this. It was all but impossible, not with Till bobbing curtsies and crying out, "God bless your ladyship," and Stubbins blubbering and attempting to kiss the ring on her left hand.

With some dismay, Freddie watched as her three newly acquired charges gathered up their various belongings.

"So," Dora said happily, "where are we going?"

"To London, I guess."

Freddie's doubtful announcement met with approval all around, Stubbins declaring he'd allus had a desire to see furrin' parts. He insisted upon carrying Freddie's portmanteau. All she had to do was make sure that he did not walk into the gates.

She heaved a deep sigh. For the first time in her life, she was entirely on her own, the mistress of her own destiny. Yet she seemed to have lost control of everything before setting foot off the estate.

She was on her way to the vast and strange city of London with scarcely a guinea to her name, having assumed the responsibility of an elderly spinster, a half-blind manservant, and a pregnant housemaid.

And the truly awful thing was that of all of them, only she seemed to possess enough wits to be terrified.

Chapter 2

The sun had the temerity to peek into the breakfast parlor before the Honorable Maxmillian Warfield took his first sip of coffee. But even the rays of morning light seemed to tiptoe past the powerful figure in the burgundy-colored dressing gown seated at the head of the dining table. His legs, encased in tan breeches, were stretched out in a negligent attitude, his broad shoulders nestled against the back of the chair. All that was visible of Mr. Warfield's head was the top of his close-cropped black hair as he perused the latest edition of the *Morning Post*.

He sipped his coffee and returned the delicate Sèvres cup to the table. The parlor maid skittered in to place Mr. Warfield's breakfast before him, one beefsteak, medium rare, two eggs cooked precisely three minutes, never less, never more, and several slices of toast, thinly buttered, absolutely no jam.

Mr. Warfield never even glanced up, and the maid slipped out unobtrusively. It was a fact completely understood by all the staff at Warfield House that no one, not even royalty, was permitted to disturb the master with a word of conversation before he had finished his breakfast.

That was why the youthful footman who entered

the parlor trembled, his throat so dry with nervousness that he could do no more than cough. The sound, slight as it was, sounded like gunshot in the chamber, silent except for the muted sounds of carriages clattering by on the London street outside.

Warfield slowly lowered the paper. He had a lean, handsome countenance with an uncompromisingly square jaw, his complexion inclined to be dark. His heavy lids gave him an expression of perpetual boredom, but when he looked up, there was no mistaking the piercing intelligence to be found in his keen gray eyes. His full lips were of a sensual cast and seemed formed to accommodate his own sardonic brand of humor.

Max stared at the footman long enough to convey the full weight of his displeasure, then barked, "Well, Bartholomew?"

The footman started and nearly dropped the silver-plated salver he carried. He clutched at the rectangle of vellum balanced on the tray, then stammered, "Th-there is a c-caller to see you, sir."

"A what!"

"A caller," Bartholomew repeated more faintly, now so pale, the freckles stood out on the bridge of his nose. "Mr. Crispin desired me to come in to tell you."

"I'll wager he did," Max said dryly. His butler was an inveterate coward.

" 'Tis a lady, sir," the footman continued. "Th-the caller, I mean."

A lady? Max arched his brow in surprise. Most of his acquaintances were familiar enough with his rigid dislike of being disturbed by anyone before noon. He could not imagine which lady might be so bold. Not even his former mistress, the tempestuous Mademoiselle Vivani, would have been that foolhardy.

"The lady is most insistent upon seeing you, sir."
Bartholomew added, "She has brought a child with
her."

"Indeed? Is she claiming it is mine?"

The footman looked much shocked. "Oh, no, I
shouldn't think so, sir. That is, I don't know." The
boy went from pale to bright red.

Max took pity upon him at last and suggested, "I
presume that is the lady's card you have there. Perhaps it would behoove us to read it?"

"Oh? Oh, yes, sir!"

Max cast down his paper and straightened in his
chair as the footman crept closer, proffering the tray
with one trembling, gloved hand. Max steadied the
salver himself before taking up the card.

He gave the inked line a cursory glance—*Lady
Arthur Bentley*.

Max grimaced and tossed the card back on the
tray. "That is no lady. It is only my sister. Tell her
to go to the deuce."

"Sir?"

"You heard me." Max vented an impatient sigh,
then amended, "Inform Lady Bentley that I do not
receive in the morning."

"Mr. Crispin already tried to tell her that, sir,"
Bartholomew said unhappily. "But the lady—your
sister is most persistent. I do not think she will go
away without seeing you."

"No, she won't!" A sharp feminine voice agreed.

Max stifled a curse as Caroline, Lady Bentley,
swept across the threshold, even the feathers on her
fashionable bonnet quivering with indignation as
she towed by the hand her youngest offspring, a girl
of three. Both mother and daughter were remarkably alike in their matching pink muslin pelisses,
their dusky curls, upturned noses, and truculent
expressions.

Lady Bentley pointed one finger dramatically at the footman, who cringed. "Maxmillian, I demand that you dismiss that creature from your service at once. And your beastly butler. Never have I been treated so shabbily. Being obliged to send in calling cards to my own brother and kept waiting in the hall as though I were some sort of tradeswoman."

Max shoved back his chair and rose lazily to his feet. "You need not blame my staff, Caroline. They were only attempting to carry out my orders. You know how I detest being disturbed before noon, and it is now . . ." He consulted his pocket watch. "Only ten forty-seven."

"But of course such an order does not apply to me! Your own sister."

Max started to assure her that it applied most particularly to her and any other of his relations, but Lady Bentley's attention had been claimed by the moppet at her side, the little girl tugging impatiently at her mother's sleeve.

While Caroline bent down to catch her daughter's lisping words, Max took the opportunity of dismissing the footman. Bartholomew backed out of the room, looking grateful to escape, and Max would have been happy to have done the same.

He had once had an old nursery governess who had told him that no matter how heartily he disliked Caroline, when he was quite grown-up, he would be very fond of his older sister. It was one of the few times that the redoubtable Nurse Roberts had ever been wrong.

Far from being pleased to see Caroline, he could only wonder what had brought her abroad at an hour when she was usually still abed sipping chocolate or fussing with her toilette. Lady Bentley never called upon him at all unless she wanted something, and whatever it was, it was generally something he would find disagreeable.

Whatever favor she desired this time, he had no intention of granting it. But he also knew there would be no getting rid of Caroline until she had her say. Eyeing his breakfast, which was getting cold, he started to demand what she wanted, but Caroline was still attempting to soothe her daughter.

"There now, Felicity love. Don't fidget so. I told you I would buy you a sweetmeat, but you must be patient while we visit Uncle Max."

"Don't want to." Felicity pouted. "Don't like Uncle Max."

"Nonsense. Now, come bid him good morrow and make your prettiest curtsy."

Max uttered a protest, but Caroline was already propelling the glowering Felicity toward him. He did not believe that he was fond of children and his niece had never done much to convince him otherwise.

But as Felicity sullenly spread her skirts, sinking into a wobbly curtsy, Max offered his hand to steady her. He was rather amused when the little girl drew his fingers toward her lips.

"You are a trifle confused, Miss Felicity. It is the gentleman who is supposed to kiss the lady's—" He broke off with a gasp as a sharp pain pierced his knuckle.

Max snatched back his hand and stared in disbelief at the raw red indentations on his finger. "She bit me!"

"Naughty Felicity," Caroline cooed. "You promised Mama not to do that anymore. Now I must scold you."

"Scold her? A good caning would be to more the purpose. She nearly drew blood. The little vixen!"

"Oh, don't make such a fuss, Max," his sister said airily. " 'Tis only a passing habit. She will outgrow it."

"Hmmph!" Max said, still nursing his injured finger. Himself, he had dark visions of Felicity someday making her debut at Almack's and sinking her fangs into Lady Jersey or one of the other patronesses of that hallowed assembly.

Caroline called upon her daughter to apologize to "dear uncle Max," but the child had already wandered off to inspect with an unholy gleam in her eye some of the china and crystal displayed upon the sideboard.

Max's unease was divided between watching Felicity's progress around the room and observing his sister stripping off her gloves and bonnet as though she intended to make a rather lengthy stay.

"And to what do I owe the honor of this invasion—I mean visit?" he demanded.

"I need to speak to you on a matter of some urgency."

"You might have just sent a note asking me to wait upon you."

"You would have ignored it."

Max was unable to refute that, and Caroline continued. "So I came when I would be sure of catching you at home. I had to venture out, in any case. Felicity has been fussing so lately that I am taking her to visit the tooth drawer."

"What a good idea," Max muttered. His niece by now had reached atop one of the pedestal cupboards and fixed her grubby little hands upon the basaltware water urn. She was in imminent danger of toppling it upon the Axminster carpet, and Caroline showed no signs of intervening or even noticing. She merely rattled on. "Of course, Nurse would

21

choose just this moment to contract a bad cold. Really, servants are so unreliable these days."

With a mumbled oath, Max strode across the room and pried Felicity away from the urn. She set up a howl, but he ignored it, seizing his niece around the waist and transporting her bodily out of the room.

In the main hall beyond, Max looked about for the parlor maid, but saw only his butler. The dapper Crispin was as ever being quite useless, lounging about, admiring himself in the pier glass.

Max strode over and thrust the screeching, kicking bundle of fury that was his niece into the man's arms. "Here. Take care of this."

Crispin's imperturbable features crumpled into an expression of dismay. "B-but, sir. What am I to do with her?"

"Stick her into the linen cupboard," Max snapped. "I don't know. Just keep the child occupied until I have managed to dispose of—to deal with her mother."

As Max strode back toward the parlor, he heard Crispin's frantic shushing noises break off into a howl as Felicity's teeth found their mark. He closed the breakfast parlor door behind him with a certain grim satisfaction. It served the cowardly butler right for letting Caroline get past him and for sending in a footman to do his job.

But his satisfaction in getting rid of his niece was fleeting. Caroline remained, and unfortunately there was no prospect of scooping her up under his arm. She had removed her pelisse and appeared undisturbed by his summary disposal of Felicity. But then, Max had frequently observed that his sister played the doting mother only during those rare half-hour intervals when her children were immediately before her.

Now she settled herself at the table and informed him in lofty accents, "You had better sit down, Max. Your breakfast is getting cold."

Max glared at her but did as she suggested, scraping back his chair with a gesture of unnecessary force. As he plunked himself down, Caroline studied his plate with a shudder. "How you can eat so much is beyond me. I am unable to choke down a morsel in the morning. It would quite upset my delicate constitution. But you might offer me a cup of coffee."

"I might," Max said. "But I won't. It would only encourage you to linger."

Caroline pouted, but then rustled over to the sideboard to the silver coffee service and helped herself, all the while complaining. "I do not know why you must ever be so surly in the morning, Max."

"I don't know either, but I am. So I wish you would simply state your business and be on your way before your she-cub causes my butler to hand in his notice."

But Caroline moved at that frustrating leisurely pace that had aggravated him ever since their nursery days. After ruining her coffee by ladening it with an inordinate amount of cream and sugar, she resumed her place at the table.

Apparently quite forgetting her delicate stomach, she plucked a piece of the toast from Max's plate and nibbled at it before getting around to explaining her latest crisis. She remarked at last with a gloomy sigh.

"Frederica has moved to London."

This portentous announcement conveyed nothing to Max.

"Frederica?" he repeated. "Am I supposed to know her?"

"Of course, you are. *Frederica Barry,*" Caroline mumbled around a mouthful of toast.

When Max continued to regard her blankly, she said, "Before her marriage, she was Frederica Jameson, that wretched girl Cousin Margaret took in after she was orphaned. Major Alex Jameson's daughter."

"Oh. You mean *Freddie.*"

Caroline pulled a face. "Yes, though I believe only you ever called her that. I am relieved to hear that you at least remember something of her."

Max remembered a great deal more than he cared to. His brow creased into a slight frown. He did not always keep a clear accounting of his various and sundry relatives. Indeed, he generally did his best to forget most of them. But Major Alexander Jameson and his daughter formed one of the better remembrances of Max's youth.

For a glorious week one autumn, this dashing major, a second cousin, had come to visit at Courtland, the principal country estate of Max's father. Although many years Max's senior, the major had not been too toplofty to bestow a great deal of attention on a young boy who often felt ignored and insignificant, being only the third son of a marquis.

For seven halcyon days, Max had hunted, rode, and fished with his great strapping cousin with the booming laugh. It had almost been enough to make Max forget his own disgrace. He had been sent down from Eton at that time, for what hellish piece of mischief Max could no longer recall.

Max's acquaintance with the major had been brief, but he had still felt a real sense of loss when several years later he had learned of the death of Alexander and his young wife in a coach accident.

Max had been but seventeen when he had journeyed down to Dorchester for the funeral. He recollected little of the service, more of what had transpired afterward when the family had gathered at the home of his Dorchester cousins. The major's now-orphaned eight-year-old daughter had been fetched there as well. But the little girl had balked at entering the mansion that was to be her new home, insisting upon being taken back to the lodgings where she had lived with Mama. Papa would never be able to find her here.

Cousin Margaret had smiled that thin smile of hers, laced with feigned indulgence. She had said, "Very well, miss. Have it your own way. But there is a storm brewing. I imagine you will be glad to come in soon enough."

But she had quite mistaken Frederica's character. Even when the rains had broken, the child had stood outside on the drive, soaked to the skin, shivering like a wet puppy. The thunder cracked, but she merely turned her small face up to the skies in defiance.

Watching out the window, Max had been inspired with a grudging admiration. When he heard Margaret bidding the governess fetch the stubborn chit inside and give her a sharp smack besides, Max had protested and gone to fetch the child himself.

Bolting down the steps of the Georgian manor, he had rolled up the collar of his greatcoat, but to no avail. He was in a fair way to being soaked himself by the time he reached Freddie.

She was a picture of abject misery, her blond curls plastered to her cheeks, the rain dripping off her chin. But when she glanced up at him, the lightning itself seemed caught in her very blue eyes.

"Are you a footman sent to carry me in?" she had demanded before he could even speak.

"No, I'm of even less importance than that. I'm

a younger son, Miss Frederica." His bitter jest only caused the child to scowl.

"My name is Fred," she said stoutly, thrusting out her thin chest. "My papa named me after the Duke of York, who was a great general."

"Well, I am Max, named after nobody in particular. I suppose I am your cousin of sorts, thrice removed."

She glared and said, "I don't care who you are. I am not going inside. Leave me alone."

"I'd be glad to do that, Fred, but I am supposed to fetch you. You might not mind being wet, but I am getting drenched, too, and I don't like it."

"Then go away. My papa will fetch me." Despite the fierceness of her tone, beneath it Max caught the threading of fear, almost desperation. Her delicate features were etched with a grief far beyond her years.

He hunkered down beside her, brushing back his rain-slicked hair. He said as gently as possible, "Freddie, I think you know that's not true. It is very sad, but your papa has had to go to heaven. That is a place quite far away. But wherever he is, I am sure he is still watching you. He would not like you being out in a storm."

She digested this in stony silence. Then her lip quivered. "But I can't go inside. I don't want this to be my new home. No one in there loves me."

"I love you, Freddie," he said solemnly, holding his arms out to her. "Come in out of the rain."

Her blue eyes searched his face earnestly for a moment. When the next boom of thunder sounded, she suddenly crumpled and flung herself into his arms, sobbing against his shoulder. Max raised her up and carried her back into the house.

He had gone to visit her many times after that day, taken her out riding in the pony cart, allowed her to hold the reins of his curricle, showed her how to climb an apple tree. It had been after that that Cousin Margaret had complained, insisting he keep his distance from the child. Margaret was doing her best to rear Frederica as a proper young lady, and a wild seventeen-year-old lad was decidedly a bad influence. Max was prepared to defy the old crone, but he had become neck deep in trouble of his own. . . . It all seemed so long ago. But it astonished him how well he still remembered Frederica, and with an unexpected stirring of tenderness.

I love you, Freddie. Come in out of the rain.

What an extraordinary thing for him to have said to the child. At the time, he had really meant those words. But he had been a much more sentimental sort of fellow in those days.

Now such feelings only made him uncomfortable, and he was quick to shrug off the memory, snap himself back to the present. He discovered that while he had been woolgathering, his sister had made further inroads upon his toast. He was alerted in time to rescue his last piece.

Unperturbed, Caroline picked up a fork and started on his eggs.

"Yes, so I do remember Frederica Jameson," he said at last. "What of it? It has been years since I saw her. She must be nearly . . ."

"Twenty-one. And already a widow."

"No one ever bothered to even tell me she had been married."

"It scarce matters now, for Frederica's husband died last autumn and she moved immediately to London," Caroline said. "She must have lived quietly for a while, for I did not know she was here until I returned to town myself in January for the Little Season. Then I discovered she had already

27

set aside her mourning and seems bent on kicking up quite a dust."

"Is she? Good for her."

Caroline paused in consuming his eggs to eye him reproachfully. "That is hardly the reaction I would have hoped for, Maxmillian."

"Isn't it? I always seemed doomed to disappoint people." Max removed his plate out of her reach. But as he picked up his own fork, he saw there was scarce enough left of the eggs to bother. With a grunt of resignation, he shoved the plate back toward his sister.

She finished off the eggs, waxing even more indignant as she detailed Freddie's further iniquities. "People are starting to say she is *fast*. Frederica has been wearing the brightest of gowns and her husband only gone these six months. She has been seen walking alone at St. James, already attending parties, playing deep at whist and—and—heaven only knows what else."

"She sounds like she is having a remarkably good time. I am glad to hear it."

"Oh, aye, *you* would be, with never a care for what gossip she might be stirring. You have raised quite a few eyebrows yourself. Though I suppose it is indelicate of me to mention it." Caroline paused to give a discreet cough.

Max had never known delicacy to prevent Caroline from saying anything she chose. He was right, for she continued. "As your sister, I ought to warn you. I know all about that infamous wager being laid, how the gentlemen are all taking bets at White's as to who your next mistress will be."

"Truly?" Max drawled. "I was not aware you were a member there. I prefer Brook's myself."

She glowered at him. "Don't be tiresome, Max. Of course I have never been inside White's. I heard about the wager when I was taking tea with Lady Ormskirk, who had it from her youngest son."

"A rattle-pated youth if there ever was one. Glad as I am to have afforded you ladies some entertainment over your tea, my dear Caroline, I feel obliged to remind you we were not discussing my peccadilloes, but Freddie's. I assume that eventually you are going to get to the point of this visit."

"The point *is* that there is every danger Frederica will create a real scandal, prove an embarrassment to the entire family."

Max grimaced. "Heaven forfend we ever cause embarrassment to the family."

"I am quite serious, Max. Any sort of bumble-broth stirred up by Frederica could prove a disaster. Have you forgotten that Elizabeth is bringing her second daughter out this season?"

"I cannot say I have been losing much sleep over that fact." Max liked his eldest sister, Eliza, even less than he did Caroline.

"And I have planned several routs and a ball of my own," Caroline said. "We simply cannot ignore Frederica. Everyone knows she is a relative of sorts. It will look most odd if she is not invited, and yet we cannot have her disgracing us all either."

"Well, what the deuce do you expect me to do about it?"

Caroline adopted that sweet, coaxing expression that Max had ever learned to mistrust. "Why, you could persuade her to return quietly to the country or go to Bath and take the waters. I hear that it is very pleasant there for widows. The Bentley family even owns a house on the Crescent that she could use. It is standing empty anyway. You could mention that to Frederica."

Max regarded his sister with patent disbelief. "You must have more maggots in your head than I ever supposed, if you think I will attempt such a thing. What makes you think the girl would listen to me?"

"Why, I believe she was once quite fond of you."

"She was eight years old then! Now she would be more likely to tell me go to the devil and mind my own business. *And* she would be in the right of it. If someone must reason with her, what is wrong with those dratted Dorchester cousins that raised her?"

Caroline sighed and proceeded to carve up the beefsteak. "Do not think that Cousin Margaret did not try. She journeyed all the way to London just for that purpose. But Frederica was positively rude to her. So ungrateful after the way the Jamesons took her in when she was left orphaned, penniless. They raised her up like one of their own daughters, arranged a brilliant match for her."

Max felt a rare stirring of curiosity. "Whom did she marry, by the by?"

"Max, you are quite impossible. Don't you ever know anything that is going on? Oh, but I forgot. You were out of the country then, still living in that barbaric place."

"The West Indies."

"Yes, just so," Caroline said vaguely, looking uncomfortable. The members of his family always did at any mention of Jamaicatown, the place where Max had acquired his fortune. They had no compunction in trying to help him spend his wealth, but none of them liked to consider the mercantile interests that were its source. It smacked too sordidly much of trade.

Caroline hastened back to the subject of Frederica. "Well, precisely two years ago, she was wed to the fifth Viscount Raincliffe."

Max, who had been taking a sip of his coffee,

choked. "Raincliffe! The fifth viscount! That elderly
rakehell. My God, he was an old rip back when I
was just a lad. He must have been ancient enough
to have been her grandfather."

"I suppose there was some difference in their
ages," Caroline conceded. "But Freddie was still
quite fortunate. A dowerless girl with little besides
a pretty face to recommend her! She could have
done far worse."

"Far worse than being forced to marry some gout-
ridden old rascal?"

"Far worse than to marry wealth and a title. And
the viscount must have left her well off, for she has
been spending money like mad. I would sell my soul
for the diamonds she wore to . . . Oh, it is entirely
too vexing. She is not behaving in the least as a
dowager viscountess should. You must stop her,
Max, before she ruins the season for all of us."

"You would do far better to appeal to our revered
brother, Harry. He is the head of the family."

"Harry!" Caroline gave a delicate snort. "He
never comes to London. Such a country bumpkin!
He might as well be some odious squire instead of
a marquis."

"Well, Edward, then. He's the bishop in the family."

"No one can listen to Ned for more than five minutes without falling asleep. No, it has to be you,
Max. No one is better at bullying people than you—
when you bestir yourself to do so."

"Thank you."

"I meant bullying them for their own good. I
heard what you did for young Tom Harker, getting
him out of that sponging house, forcing him to give
up gaming and join a cavalry regiment. His mother
declares that you quite saved Tom's life."

"She quite exaggerates. I never put myself to

that much trouble for anyone, although I do actually like Tom Harker. Despite his wild streak, he is a young man of great merits, his chief one being that he is no relation of mine."

Caroline pouted. "You take such delight in vexing me. Does this mean you utterly refuse to do anything about Frederica?"

"Your understanding, my dear sister, is, as ever, acute."

"And so our family is to be humiliated by her antics, the season ruined, and you will not care a jot! In all my twenty-nine years, I have never known anyone as selfish."

"Twenty-nine? But I was thirty-three last Michaelmas. That should make you—"

"Never mind," Caroline said, turning an angry shade of red. "I should have known you would be disobliging."

"So you should have. It would have saved us both a deal of bother, and I might have gotten to eat my own breakfast."

She shoved back her chair and huffed to her feet.

"What! You are going?" he mocked. "There is still half the beefsteak left."

"Don't be horrid. I told you I cannot eat in the mornings. And with all this upset over Frederica, I am likely to become quite ill. Indeed, I feel a spasm coming on already."

But since she made this announcement in very hearty accents, Max saw no cause for alarm. She flounced over and jerked on her pelisse, gloves, and finally her bonnet.

Max, who had also risen, reached out to help her straighten it but received a sharp rap across the knuckles for his pains. Seeing how agitated she was, Max relented enough to offer some rare brotherly advice.

"You need to cultivate a thicker skin, Caro. If the old tabbies want to wag their tongues over Freddie, let them."

"That is all very well for you to say." She sniffed. "When that dreadful girl creates a scandal and people start to cut us, I daresay you won't even notice. But what if I send out the cards to my ball and no one comes?"

"Then the devil with them. Close up your house and take a holiday. I have it on excellent authority that Bath is a very nice place."

His sister shot him such a look, Max felt glad she no longer had the carving knife within reach. Turning on her heel, Caroline stormed toward the door, spurning him with an imperious wave of her hand.

"Do not attempt to accompany me out, Maxmillian. I am seriously displeased with you."

"I shall endeavor not to be crushed."

She entirely missed his ironic bow as she slammed the parlor door behind her. The last he heard of her was in the front hall, demanding that Crispin unhand her darling child at once.

Max grinned. He supposed he ought to be ashamed for baiting his sister. Ought to be, but wasn't. Caroline deserved whatever she got for bursting in upon him with her brat at this hour.

And what she had gotten had been a damn fine breakfast, Max thought ruefully, observing what little remained on his plate. He sank back down in his chair to the comforts of half a beefsteak and a cold cup of coffee.

He thought of summoning Crispin and ordering up a fresh plate, but he found he had little appetite. That was always the way of it whenever his routine was interrupted.

The devil take Caroline anyway for disturbing what had been an otherwise peaceful morning, and all to no purpose. She should have known he would never agree to her ridiculous request. Perhaps he was as selfish as she said, but then, he never pretended to be otherwise.

He had long ago arranged his life entirely to his own satisfaction. That was the great reward of being both wealthy and a confirmed bachelor. His family often took a different view of the matter, but his acid tongue kept most of them from badgering him for favors. Most of them except for Caroline. What cork-brained notions she was always entertaining, and this latest one topped them all! Expecting him to meddle in the doings of little Freddie Jameson.

Although, he supposed, she was not that little anymore. In spite of himself, he could not help wondering. What sort of woman had she grown up to be, that stubborn, spirited child? He tried to picture her as a lady, a wife, a widow, but his mind refused to make the leap. He could envision her only as that wistful-eyed moppet clinging to his hand whenever he had to turn her over to the Jamesons' governess after one of their outings.

He had promised her he would continue to visit her often. But it had been a promise he had been unable to keep. He remembered he had tried to write her a letter explaining. But how did one explain to an eight-year-old child a tale of passion gone awry, the youthful madness that had brought him dishonor and a perhaps well-deserved exile to a land both foreign and far away? He had torn the letter up before he had written more than the greeting.

Not that it signified. Doubtlessly Freddie had forgotten him swiftly enough. Without her wild cousin Max to corrupt her, she had likely grown to be an accomplished young lady, captivating enough to secure for herself a viscount, though it still disturbed Max to think of her marrying that disgusting old roué.

In any case, she was well off now, a wealthy widow, a position that gave her some measure of freedom if only she had the good sense not to take it too far. And if she didn't?

Then perhaps someone ought to shake some sense into the young woman. But, thank God, it was not his place to do so. Simply because he had been kind to her once, made her some half-baked promises in the sentimental folly of his youth, there was no reason he should feel responsible or even guilty for never having inquired after her in all these years. In the interval, he had learned a great deal of wisdom, most particularly to avoid anyone likely to disturb his comfortable existence.

Leaning back in his chair, he unfolded his newspaper and attempted to dismiss all thoughts of Freddie, recapture the peace and solitude he had been enjoying before Caroline had burst in upon him.

But it was the most aggravating thing imaginable. He could not seem to focus on the inkprint. Having resurrected Frederica's memory, he could not restore it to the ashes where it belonged. As stubborn as Freddie herself, the image persisted in swimming through his mind.

The image of a little girl swallowed up by a threatening sky, her tears mingling with the rain.

Chapter 3

The mansion beyond the high screen wall glowed like a bright beacon, candlelight spilling through the windows upon the press of carriages lining up on the winding drive. The vehicles paused in turn before the imposing Palladian-style manor, depositing their occupants at the doorstep. Ladies whose jewels winked in the moonlight, gentlemen in their high crown beavers all drifted up the stairs toward the lights and music.

To Freddie, they looked like a parcel of giddy moths fluttering through the darkness toward a beckoning flame. Huddling deeper in the satiny folds of her cloak, she peered between the bars of the iron gate. She could feel the tension between her shoulder blades as she judged the chaos of the arriving guests, awaiting the right moment to make her move.

Dora crowded close behind her, the tall, ungainly woman easily able to see over Frederica's head.

"Oooh, 'tis just like fairyland," she breathed in a hiss loud enough to have done credit to a stage villain.

"Shhh!" Freddie said, placing a cautioning finger to her lips.

Dora nodded, but even in the shadows Freddie could see the way the woman's brown eyes shone with excitement. After six months of struggling to survive in the vast, cold city of London, it still all seemed like a grand adventure to Dora. Nothing daunted her. Not the creditors beating upon their door, nor that their money was nearly gone, nor that the larder was practically empty.

They had dined that evening upon boiled cabbage and tough chicken. Dora had made merry jests about how the poor thing had sacrificed its life in vain. With a hungry rumble yet sounding in her stomach, Freddie wished she found their situation equally amusing.

As the two women studied the distant mansion, it was Dora who tried to crowd closer to the gate, Dora who nearly trod upon Freddie's toes in her eagerness.

" 'Tis all so grand." She sighed. "Lord and Lady Channing must be quite rich."

"Yes," Freddie agreed.

"The ball is going to be wonderful, quite the event of the season."

"Yes," Freddie said.

"What a pity you weren't invited."

"Yes."

"It would be so magnificent to be able to go in through the *front* door."

"Yes," Freddie repeated glumly. Of course, if her scheme went awry, she might be seeing the front door far sooner than she wished. For a moment, she desired nothing more than to be able to walk away and forget the whole thing. But propelled by a combination of desperation and determination, she stepped back from the gates, whispering, "All right. The house appears crowded enough to risk it. Let's go."

Freddie set off without looking back. Clinging close to the wall, she rounded the corner, staying well out of the lamplight spilling on the pavement. It would not do for any of the other arriving guests to see the Dowager Viscountess of Raincliffe creeping about the streets like a footpad.

That might entirely put an end to the rumors that she had been left a wealthy widow, convenient rumors that had secured her a great deal of credit. Tradesmen who thought she was merely forgetful about paying her bills might not be nearly so forbearing if the truth were bandied abroad.

But as she slipped along, following the stone wall, she noted that her stealth was entirely wasted. Dora, hard on her heels, lumbered along, crackling twigs beneath her feet, panting a little from the exertion of keeping up.

When they reached the back of the mansion, the wall became lower, closing off the gardens from the bustle of the London streets. Dora reached out to pluck at Freddie's cloak, the woman trembling now as much from nervousness as excitement.

"I—I have been reconsidering, Freddie. Perhaps this is not such a good idea. It would be so humiliating if you were caught. Perhaps the Channings might even send for the constable and—and after all, we were invited to Mrs. Pomfret's. Such a very sweet lady. We should go there instead."

"I've already explained to you, Dora. We are getting nowhere with me playing at whist with old ladies for a penny a point. If we are even going to pay the rent this month, I need to sit in on a game of higher stakes."

"But you have never been to the Channings. Perhaps they don't game at all."

"Nonsense. That is all they do at affairs like this, play cards, waltz, and eat."

"Oh, waltzing! That would be so agreeable."

"So would eating," Freddie said tartly. "But I am afraid we have other business to accomplish first."

A sparkle of sudden tears glinted in Dora's eyes. For such a stolid-looking female, she was an excessively emotional creature. She sniffed. "It should not be this way, you so young and left a widow to fend for yourself. Why, you are not much older than the young ladies making their debut this Season. You should be attending the ball tonight, going in by the front door, all gowned in white like an angel, with me as your chaperone, a grand lady . . .

"A grand *married* lady," she added with a quiver in her voice. "I would be bringing you out in society, introducing you to eligible partners. You would be the toast of the season, so carefree with all the gentlemen flocking around you. You would flirt, sip champagne, and then that certain one would appear far more handsome and gallant than all the rest, and you—"

"Oh, please, Dora," Freddie interrupted. The wistfulness in Dora's voice touched off an unexpected answering chord in her own heart. She had almost become caught up in Dora's vision, and that seemed somehow disloyal to Leon to be having such dreams, regrets, wishes that her life had proceeded upon different lines.

"It would be dreadfully boring," she said. "I fear I have always been destined to be more of a hellborn babe than anyone's angel. Besides, the pair of us came to London to be wicked women, remember?"

"Oh, yes." Dora sighed. "I keep forgetting."

"Being respectably invited to the Channings' party would be so tame. This way will be infinitely more exciting."

But Freddie was not certain whom she was trying to convince, herself or Dora, as she gazed at the wall looming before her. It was not so high as in the front and the brickwork uneven enough to afford her a toehold. But the challenge would be to get over it unseen or without arriving in a totally disheveled state.

Compressing her lips, she stripped off her cloak and handed it to Dora. As Freddie straightened her mameluke turban adorned with white ostrich feathers, she noticed Dora regarding her with a frown.

"What is the matter? Do I not look all right?" She spread out the folds of her India muslin gown, the gilt spangles shimmering even in the semi-darkness. Although the strings of her stays might be a little frayed, at least outwardly she was the picture of elegance, owing to the services of a little modiste who was too flattered by the patronage of a viscountess to worry about dilatory payments.

Though of late, Freddie often felt as if she would have traded all the silks on her back for a good roast beef dinner. The butcher and greengrocer had not proved near as tolerant as her seamstress.

Pacing closer, Dora continued to study the new gown and scowl. "It's that turban," she pronounced at last. "It's too *old* for you, and the skirts of the gown are far too full for the current fashion."

"Oh, *that.*" Freddie shrugged. "My dear Dora, you know the necessity for the turban and the full skirts as well as I do."

Dora nodded her agreement, but looked none too happy about it. "What if someone notices when you try to— Oh, dear, I wish you would let me come with you."

"That would only increase the chance of detection. If this goes awry, there is no sense both of us

40

ending in Newgate." Freddie gave her a quick smile, feeling vaguely guilty as she offered this excuse. Dora was a perfect dear, but the truth was, Freddie found the woman something of a detriment when she was playing cards. Dora had a tendency to hover at Freddie's shoulders, her candid eyes lighting up when Freddie drew a good hand, biting her nails whenever Freddie attempted to bluff.

Before Dora could argue with her, Freddie took the woman by the arm, urging her on her way. "Now, we have stood here whispering long enough. Get along with you before someone comes. Secure a hackney cab and wait for me at the corner over there. I will meet you in a couple of hours."

She gave Dora a nudge, hustling her on her way, but not so briskly that she failed to call softly after her. "And, Dora . . . have a care for yourself."

"Pooh!" Dora said stoutly. Grinning, she produced a pearl-handled pistol from beneath the depths of her shawl and waved it recklessly about. "Don't worry about me. I am more than a match for any rascal lurking in the dark."

"For heaven's sake," Freddie hissed. "Watch where you are aiming that thing."

But Dora had already plunged off into the shadows, her attempts to slink along all but ludicrous. With a mixture of amusement and anxiety, Freddie watched her disappear. There could be no more naive woman in all of London than Theodora Applegate. She was so trusting, she would surrender her pistol to the nearest footpad if he but politely asked to admire the handle.

Freddie wished that Dora would have stayed safely at home, but there had been no way to compel her to do so. Dora could be amazingly obstinate. In truth, it was the height of foolhardiness for either one of them to be skulking about the streets at night, even in London's elegant Mayfair district. But necessity, Freddie had often found, frequently obliged one to act the fool.

Keeping to the darkness, she stood close to the wall, trying to summon up the final burst of courage that would carry her over it. A night breeze wafted to her the scent of roses from the garden, the heady perfume seeming somehow bound up with the distant lilt of violins. But rather than enticing her, the sound of a waltz filled her with an odd melancholy.

She never had learned to perform the modern dance. Her aunt had not approved of it, and Leon had preferred the stately minuets and spritely cotillions of his own youth. The waltz seemed so much more daring, so romantic. But after all, she had not come here for the dancing.

Shivering a little in the night air, Freddie nervously fingered her necklace. Her diamonds were long gone, cleverly copied with paste imitations, likewise the sapphire aigrette affixed to her turban. The only thing that seemed genuine about her was the hollow feeling in the pit of her stomach.

Leon had always declared it possible for a man to live handsomely by his wits alone in the vast city of London. But Freddie was coming to the conclusion that she must not possess as much of that particular commodity as her late husband.

She had begun to feel wearied, a little overwhelmed by the mounting list of her creditors, weighed down with her responsibilities. Sometimes she longed to give up and just flee, though she scarce knew where. She was always restrained by the knowledge that she no longer had just herself to consider. For the first time in her life, she had people dependent upon her, people who actually believed in her abilities to accomplish miracles; dear, foolish Dora, the nearsighted Stubbins now elevated to the position of butler, fiercely proud of his keys to the wine cellar, although they scarce had a single bottle to rack there. And Till, that sweet, timid housemaid who had been seduced and abandoned, had given birth to the most darling baby girl only two months before.

They all, even the babe, seemed to regard Freddie with misplaced adoration, as though she were some sort of heroine, Joan of Arc and Lady Bountiful rolled into one. Their blind faith in her both touched and terrified Freddie.

What if she let them down? What if she got them all arrested for debt or worse? What if—

No, she could not continue this line of thinking or in another moment she would lose heart altogether and flee from the Channings' mansion like the veriest coward.

She must be calm, harbor only optimistic thoughts. What if she won a fortune at the tables tonight? It had been known to happen, especially at these sort of wealthy parties where people frequently played for high stakes.

Men had also been known to retire from these events utterly ruined and go home to blow their brains out. The thought crept in unbidden. Seeking to quell it, Freddie was only partly successful.

She felt a fluttering beneath her rib cage, but she stripped off her gloves, slipping them into the pocket concealed by the folds of her gown. Stepping close to the wall, she listened intently, trying to discern if any one of the Channings' guests might have been tempted to take a moonlight stroll in the gardens.

She heard nothing but the gentle rustling of leaves, the distant sounds of music and laughter spilling from the house beyond. She drew in a deep breath. It was now or never.

"Ah, well, champagne and roses tonight," she muttered. "Disgrace and debtor's prison tomorrow. If all else fails, we can flee to the Continent. I daresay Dora would like to see Paris."

Freddie examined the wall, feeling for her first toehold. It was time to see if all those years of defying Aunt Jameson's injunction against climbing were about to pay off.

Chapter 4

The hostess of one of the most highly attended routs of the season should not have been stealing into the garden with any man, let alone one not her husband. But Lady Lavinia Channing had always been a little reckless with her reputation.

Yet the lady was well over thirty, Max Warfield thought as he ducked to avoid a low-hanging branch. She was experienced enough to be fly to the time of day and certainly old enough to look out for herself. It was more likely he who should be wary, Max admonished himself with a wry crook of his lips as he followed his hostess to a sequestered spot behind some of the rosebushes.

Perhaps he should not have chosen to attend this particular affair at all. He rarely ever attended such balls, finding the throngs of people, the fluttering debutantes, the empty conversation, all rather tedious. Yet the Channings' parties were certainly livelier than most and the hostess most charming.

But his presence here was only giving Lavinia Channing ideas, and Lord knows, the lady already had enough of those. He had welcomed her suggestion to step outside for a breath of air. It had been infernally hot in the ballroom and he had hardly expected Lavinia to be bold enough to attempt a tryst with him in her husband's own gardens.

But his hostess had clearly selected Max for the role of Adam in this Garden of Eden. And this particular Eve was quite tempting, possessed of a most lovely set of apples. Having put a respectable distance between them and the French doors leading out from the ballroom, the light pooling onto the garden walkway, Lavinia turned to face him.

Her lush breasts seemed to strain against the confines of her low-necked gown, the gauzy fabric almost scandalously transparent. Moonlight haloed her crown of dark curls, outlining the sensual cast of her slanted eyes and full lips.

Max knew that Lady Channing was the odds-on favorite to be his next mistress ever since he had parted company with that temperamental virago Vivani. And he could scarce deny Lavinia's full-blown attraction. She was exactly as he preferred his women, with no pretensions to innocence and possessed of a lusty sense of humor.

Yet for all that, even when her lips parted invitingly, he made no move to fulfill her expectations by taking her into his embrace.

Rather, he folded his arms across his chest and quirked one brow in mocking fashion. "Well, so now we have had our little stroll. Shouldn't we be getting back?"

She smiled. "Do not be so provoking, Max. You cannot believe I brought you out here to admire my hydrangea bushes. Kiss me."

He bent forward and obliged, bestowing a light peck on her cheek.

She pulled a face. "I could have gotten that much from my brother."

"Or your husband?"

"Ah!" Her face lit up with sudden comprehension. "Is that all that has been restraining you?"

"One of my trifling scruples, my dear. I admit I don't have many of them, but I rather stick at involving myself with a married woman. Jealous husbands are the very devil, full of the most annoying suggestions, such as pistols at dawn. And I do hate having my morning routine disturbed."

She gave a tinkling laugh. "You need have no fear of my George. I doubt he has ever bestirred himself to see the sunrise in the whole of his life. Besides, he takes little notice of my—er—social activities. He is a most complacent sort of husband."

Max only shrugged. He found the complacent ones worse than the jealous sort and far more difficult to comprehend. "I am flattered by your interest, my lady," he said, "but I have my own peculiar code. Never to drive my high perch phaeton when I am foxed, never to trade fisticuffs with anyone half my weight, and never to bed a married lady."

"Then what do you expect me to do?" Lavinia pouted. "Poison poor George and bury him 'neath the delphiniums?"

"Given the size of Lord Channing, I doubt he'd fit so tidily in a flower bed. Alas, my lady. I fear there is little to be done but return discreetly to the ballroom."

Max stepped back, sweeping her a mock gallant bow, waiting for her to glide past him. But discretion was not one of Lavinia's strong points. Nor was giving up so easily.

Instead of skirting by, she brushed provocatively against him, her closeness affording him a full view down the front of her bodice. She murmured, "Maybe I don't wish to return to the house so soon. And maybe you don't want me to either." She ran one finger lightly against the sensitive skin beneath his eye, touching upon a recent bruise that was still tender. He winced.

Her lips curved in a sly smile. "I heard about what happened at Gentleman Jackson's yesterday when you were taking your sparring exercise. The great Max Warfield, so noted for his ability at fisticuffs, allowing a greenhorn to slip in a hit past his guard.

"What happened to the famous Warfield concentration?" she teased. "Could it be you were thinking of me?"

Max scowled. No, he had been thinking about an eight-year-old girl, but he was not about to confess that to Lady Channing. He was annoyed enough by the remembrance of the incident at the sparring salon, even more annoyed to hear it was being bruited about. His concentration *had* slipped. Little Freddie Jameson kept leaping into his head at the most damnably inconvenient times ever since Caroline's intrusion at his breakfast table yesterday morning.

After he had had his eye clipped by a raw youth, Max had nearly decided to go see the girl after all, if for no other reason than to exorcise Freddie from his thoughts. But something had held him back. Perhaps it had been a fear of what he might find. He cherished so few of his memories, but he did rather have a fancy for the one of that sprite of a girl, her liveliness and quick wit reflected in her dancing blue eyes. It would be cursed disappointing to discover that she had been molded into just another fashionable female with cotton for brains.

But perhaps the stronger motive holding him back from calling on Freddie was a vague sense of guilt, which was both irritating and ridiculous. Why should he continue to feel any sort of responsibility just because he had once plucked the girl out of a storm?

"Pure foolishness," Max muttered. He did not realize he had spoken aloud until Lavinia Channing responded in purring tones. "Do you really think so?"

Max snapped back to his surroundings with a start, realizing that Lavinia had taken advantage of his inattention to wrap her arms around his neck, insinuating herself close against him.

"Ah, Max, you were woolgathering again." She chuckled. "This is getting to be a dangerous habit. I fear that now even I can pop a hit past your guard."

So saying, she tugged his head down, her lips crashing against his own. Her mouth was hot and accomplished enough that Max felt an inevitable stirring of masculine response. He caught himself kissing her back, and there was no saying where this idiocy would have led him, when he was startled by the crackling of a twig. Contrasted to the soft hush of the garden, the distant lilt of music from the ballroom, it had about the same effect as the snap of a whip.

Max's head jerked upward. As he strained, listening, peering into the darkness of the trees, a loud rustling caught his attention, coming from the opposite end of the garden near the wall.

"What the—" he exclaimed, his startled gaze focusing on the shadowy form that was taking on a more distinct shape.

"Mmmm," Lavinia murmured, snuggling closer, her hands creeping beneath his frock coat to caress his chest through the fabric of his white silk waistcoat.

"Behave yourself, Lavinia," he hissed, trying to still her busy hands. "We are not alone."

"Don't be absurd, darling. Of course we are." She pressed hot, hungry kisses along the line of his jaw.

"No!" he insisted, though he could scarce credit his own eyes. "There—there appears to be a dowager in a turban scaling your garden wall."

"What!"

He succeeded in capturing Lavinia's attention at last. She broke off in mid-kiss and whipped about to peer behind her.

Moonlight shimmered on the folds of a spangled gown, two white slippers flailing the air for a second, until the strange woman dropped down with a soft thud, staggering to keep her balance.

Max dodged farther back behind the bushes, pulling Lady Channing with him.

"Oh, bother," she whispered. "I bribed my footman heavily to make sure no guests came out through the garden doors to spy upon us. Who would have thought that one of the old tabbies would possess enough enterprise to climb the wall?"

"I doubt this is one of your guests," Max said. He tensed, peering between the branches of the leaves. The conduct of the strange woman was no less furtive than his own. She looked quickly from side to side and began creeping forward along the cobbled path.

"Be still, Lavinia," he said when Lady Channing shifted restively at his side. "I think we are about to capture a most daring thief."

"A thief? Wearing diamonds?"

As the woman tiptoed through the garden and glided within yards of where he hid, Max had to admit there had never been a less likely-looking burglar. He still could not obtain a clear view of her face, but something about her caused him to assess his initial estimate of her age. Her figure was far too lithe, her step too quick for an old woman.

She paused just outside the circle of light spilling through the French doors to calmly pull on her gloves. Then, bold as any West End doxy, she headed for the house. Max caught just a glimpse of a youthful countenance, a hint of golden curl wisping from beneath the turban before he started forward, intending to apprehend her.

He was surprised when Lady Channing restrained him.

"No, Max. Let her go."

"Let her go? You're going to permit some stranger to enter your house? Diamonds or not, she might still intend to walk off with your silver."

"I don't think so." Lady Channing smothered a soft trill of laughter. "I recognize her. It is the Merry Widow."

"Who?"

"The Merry Widow. That is the nickname everyone has been giving the Dowager Viscountess of Raincliffe."

Dowager Viscountess of— Max felt as if he had taken a sudden swift kick to the gut. That very odd female scrambling over the wall, slinking through the garden had been . . . Frederica Jameson?

He whirled around, staring at the spot where he had last seen her, but of course she had already disappeared, vanished as though she were as much of an apparition as those phantom memories that had been plaguing him of late.

"That's absurd," he told Lady Channing uncertainly. "What would Freddie— I mean, what would Lady Raincliffe be doing sneaking through your garden?"

"Trying to find a way to get into my party, I suppose. Poor dear. She need not have gone to such trouble. I would have invited her, but your sister, that is, Lady Bentley, told me not to bother."

"Did she, by God!"

"Yes. She said the viscountess is far too sickly to be accepting so many invitations. That Lady Raincliffe would likely be departing for Bath very soon."

Max grimaced. Either Caroline had placed too much faith in her abilities to coax Max into interfering, or his sister had devised some plan of her own to send Freddie packing.

He said, "You should know better than to place much confidence in anything Caroline might say."

"Obviously." Lavinia's eyes twinkled with amusement. "Not only does the viscountess appear quite hale, but excessively athletic."

"Indeed," Max agreed without really paying much heed to what she was saying. Frowning, he paced toward the house.

Lavinia fell into step beside him. "She is a cousin of yours, isn't she, this little widow? At least that was what Caroline led me to believe."

"Frederica is a relative of sorts," Max said slowly. "I have not seen her for years, since she was a child, in fact."

"Then I suppose I had best take you inside and see that you become reacquainted. You appear far too distracted to resume what we were doing. Ah, well, perhaps I did choose my moment unwisely. But you are a difficult man to catch alone."

She looked up at him, flashing her glinting smile. "Another time, another place, perhaps?"

Max knew he should set her straight about that at once. He never made the mistake of letting the same opponent get past his guard. But instead, he made some noncommittal reply. Lady Channing was quite right. He was distracted. Freddie's sudden and startling appearance had unsettled him in a way he could not explain.

All he knew was that having earlier decided that he did not want to see her, he now felt afire with curiosity, impatient to rush into the ballroom and have a good look at the Dowager Viscountess Raincliffe.

He took such long strides, Lavinia had difficulty keeping up with him. But by the time they emerged beneath the arch of the blue and gilt ballroom, she had managed to link her arm through his in a possessive fashion.

He should have discouraged the gesture, but he was too busy scanning the assembled throng for some sign of Freddie, mentally cursing the fact that Lavinia had seen fit to invite so blasted many people.

The crush was so complete, there was scarce room for dancing. Couples moving through the measures of a quadrille nearly trod the toes of the stately matrons attempting to keep an eye on their charges.

Max began inching his way forward through the press of people. Lady Channing clung to his arm, firing off gracious remarks to some of her other guests.

She still managed to find time to whisper to Max behind the screen of her fan. "Of course, you realize this little cousin of yours has been causing quite a stir, having put off her mourning and begun amusing herself a little too soon."

So Caroline had already said. As usual, Max had assumed that his sister's reports were greatly exaggerated. But what he had seen of Freddie's behavior so far was hardly reassuring.

Craning his neck, he spotted her bare yards away, holding court in the shadow of one of the ballroom's tall marble pillars. Freddie had wasted little time in making herself at home, sipping a glass of lemonade. She was surrounded by a throng of gentlemen in their black evening coats. They buzzed around her like a hive full of drones guarding a honey pot.

Max's first impression was that she seemed very much the little girl he remembered, gotten up in Mother's clothes, that turban too large for her. Upon closer inspection, he noted the plump peach of her cheeks had faded to a complexion of flawless ivory, the snub nose had somehow taken an aquiline turn, the babe-soft face molded into one of delicate and dazzlingly feminine proportions.

The once-stubborn little mouth curved into generous berry red lips. And her figure . . . If the turban was large, the gown was not, hugging to perfection the high, pert outline of her breasts. There was no trace of the girl-child left in her willowy form, only the evidence of a woman grown.

Max stared, shot through with an unexpected pang of melancholy. Lavinia bent close to him to murmur, "Ah, I see the viscountess has attracted her usual court."

Max managed to wrench his gaze from Freddie, taking note of the males clustered around her. Stanway, Whitby, Fremont, and Burke.

He frowned. "Good God. She seems to have gathered up every fortune hunter within a fifty-mile radius of London."

He moved purposefully forward. Most of the gentlemen bore the sense to clear a path for Max and Lady Channing, but he was obliged to elbow his way in front of Mr. Burke. The slick, sandy-haired fop emitted a protest which Max ignored.

Freddie had been laughing at something the portly Lord Stanway had said. But she straightened, glancing in Max's direction. Her eyes were still that same perfect shade of blue, though the gold-tipped lashes seemed more lush. Yet she looked out at the world with the same expression, that mingling of boldness and wariness, as though she expected to be hurt but defied anyone to try to harm her.

Max wondered if it was possible she would recognize him after all these years. For a moment he thought she did, for some of the color ebbed from her cheeks. Then he realized her gaze had shifted to the woman pressed so close to his side. It was not he who caused Freddie's hand to flutter nervously, toy with her necklace, but Lavinia.

Then Frederica seemed to rally. She sank into a graceful curtsy, forcing a broad smile to her lips.

"Why, Lady Channing, there you are at last. I— I have been looking for you. So rude you must be thinking me, not even to greet my hostess. But I arrived late owing to the press of carriages. This London traffic, my dear! Too dreadful. I declare, it gets worse all the time."

It was the most brazen performance Max had ever seen, Freddie's fear betrayed only in the candid depths of her eyes. He was sore tempted to break into applause, but he was a little tense himself, uncertain what Lavinia meant to do.

But Lavinia also smiled brilliantly, slipping into her own part with equal ease. "My dear viscountess, there is not the least need to apologize. I am only too delighted to see you here. I had greatly feared my invitation to you might have gone astray."

Frederica did have the grace to blush a little at that. "Your ladyship is too kind."

Apparently relieved of her apprehension of being escorted to the door, Freddie turned her attention back to Max. She studied him more earnestly this time, a faint crease appearing between the delicate arch of her brows.

"Dear viscountess," Lavinia cooed. "I am placed in the awkward position of introducing you to someone you already know. The Honorable Mr. Maxmillian Warfield."

Freddie half extended her hand, and Max took it, waiting, for he scarce knew what. A flicker of something—perhaps recognition at last—appeared in Frederica's eyes. Her fingers trembled. But then she lowered her lashes, withdrawing her hand. Her smile was so distant, he was left to wonder if he had imagined any other response.

"Good evening, Mr. Warfield," she said. "Yes, I am acquainted with some people by that name. Distant cousins, I believe, of the Marquis of Huntley branch of the family. Principal estate, Courtland Park in Derbyshire. Would you be one of those Warfields?"

"One of those?" Max echoed, strangely irritated. She made it sound as if she were reading out of the social register. "Yes, I am. In fact, I am the cousin who used to call upon you when you lived in Dorchester. I took you out riding in the pony cart."

"Did you? Why, how handsome of you. You must forgive my not remembering. It is so difficult to recollect events that happened when one was only eight years old."

She turned aside to wave to an elderly gallant who approached, his bristling mustaches every bit as gray as the rows of curls on his old-fashioned tye wig.

"Ah, here is the gentleman I have been waiting for. I am promised to General Fortescue for the next dance. I do trust all of you will excuse me."

And before Max could say another word, Frederica glided away on the arm of General Sir Mordant Fortescue, oblivious to the grumblings of all her younger gallants left in the lurch.

And Max was disconcerted to find that he was as disappointed as any of them. So that was all there was to his meeting Freddie Jameson again after all these years! She didn't even remember him. Of course, he assured himself that he had never been unreasonable enough to expect otherwise. Then what was he making such a bother about? Just because he had thought perhaps some sort of special bond had existed between them. What rubbish!

She had been only a child. Indeed, when he had gone away, he had hoped that she would forget him. Why then did he feel so piqued that she had done just that? Piqued and even though he was loathe to admit it, a little . . . hurt?

Hurt! Maxmillian Warfield? Never! He was long past anyone being able to accomplish such a thing. He gave himself a sharp mental shake to clear his head. If he indulged in any more such fuddled notions, he might even be drummed out of the care-for-nobody society of which he considered himself a member in good standing.

He became aware that Lavinia was trying to claim his attention, telling him that it was his dance. Whether it was or not, waltzing with her seemed as good a way to pass his time as any.

Resting one hand lightly on her trim waist, clasping her hand with the other, he set off down the ballroom. Max knew he was not the most inspired dancer, but at least he kept good steady time. He felt better now that he had seen Frederica. His curiosity had been satisfied. He could stop thinking about her.

Having come to this conclusion, he spent the next several twirls about the ballroom trying to see which of the other couples might be Frederica and General Fortescue.

He continued to do so without success until Lavinia complained, "Max. Halloo! I am down *here*, Max."

"What?" He frowned, glancing down at her, not even certain what she had just said. "Oh, yes, certainly. Your ball is going quite splendidly. You have outdone yourself as usual, my lady."

Then he went back to looking for Frederica, twisting his head in various directions, half dancing, half pulling Lavinia along with him.

"She isn't dancing, Max," Lavinia said, more loudly this time to be sure of claiming his attention.

"I—I beg your pardon?"

"I said, your pretty little cousin isn't dancing. She and General Fortescue appear to have decided to sit this one out."

Max was mortified, partly because Lady Channing should so easily have guessed what he was doing and partly because his lack of concentration caused him to tread upon her toes.

"My apologies," he said gruffly, but other concerns crowded uppermost to his mind. "Where on earth could Freddie and that old roué have gone? A fine set she appears to have taken up with. Fortune hunters and then a miserable loose screw like Mordy Fortescue. One would think she would have had enough of that sort of thing with her late husband."

"One would think," Lavinia replied in accents of long-suffering patience.

Max whipped her around in a dizzying circle as he tried to scan all sides of the room at once. "Surely Freddie has better sense than to slip off alone with an unconscionable rogue like that."

Lavinia sighed. "Does she? I don't know. But if you are going to continue looking like a stern papa who has caught the footman tweaking his daughter's garters, perhaps you had better go look for your Freddie."

She came to a stop and began to ease herself out of his grasp. Max suddenly realized what an ass he must appear. He tightened his grip and apologized, making an effort to take some heed of his partner.

"I am sorry. Of course, I don't want to go look for her. It is just—" What was it just? Damned if he knew himself what was causing him to behave so oddly. He finished lamely, "Frederica is a relative of sorts. One feels a little responsible."

"Maybe *one* does, but not Max Warfield." Lavinia glanced up at him through narrowed eyes. "You are the only person I have ever met who wishes he was born an orphan. 'Fess up, Max. What is your real interest in the girl?"

"I already told you."

"Oh, yes, you used to know her when she was eight years old. Well, she obviously isn't eight anymore. She's grown to be a beautiful woman with a handsome figure and a complexion that makes me want to hate her. And you . . . perhaps you are harboring some notions like Burke and those others of dangling for a rich wife."

Max gave a snort. "I am not dangling for a wife, rich or otherwise."

"Good." She smiled. "Not that it matters to me. I assure you, I have no scruples about forming liaisons with married men. But you might be severely disappointed in your widow. I have heard something, just a rumor, mind you, from a dear friend who knows the Raincliffe family intimately. She believes that far from being left wealthy, Frederica was cut out of the old man's will, and that his heirs promptly turned her out of doors."

"Foolish gossip," Max growled. "I trust you will not go about repeating it."

"Oh, no," Lavinia said, lowering her lashes demurely. "It would not at all amuse me to do so. At the moment."

Max started to demand what she meant by that. But the dance ended and it became her parting shot. She rustled away to be claimed by her next partner.

With a mighty scowl Max watched her go. There was no real harm in Lavinia. But she could be teasing, exasperating, with as sharp claws as any female. If there was one thing he had no patience for, it was petticoat intrigue. He fervently wished he had spent his evening in far more sensible fashion, in the totally masculine world of his club.

It only added to his aggravation that he was doing the very thing he had sworn to his sister Caroline he would not do, take an interest in the affairs of Frederica Jameson. He determined anew to put her out of his head and succeeded rather better this time.

He located Mr. Leith Garson and Sir Pollack Sprague by the punch bowl, acquaintances of his from the Corinthian set he favored. He was soon lost in a conversation regarding the curricle race Mr. Garson was slated to run the next week. Max's humor improved enough that he even pledged himself to Sir Pollack for the next morning. Sprague was thinking of purchasing a new hack, and he desired Max's opinion of the beast.

Pleasantly occupied, it was nigh on midnight before Max caught another glimpse of Freddie. He paused to peek into the parlor, which had been set aside for cards. He looked in with no real interest. He always found both cards and the dice too sedentary an activity. Any wagering he did involved more active sport, a prizefight, a horse race, a cricket match.

Besides, the players gathered around the green baize tables at the Channings appeared a most uninteresting lot, mostly the older gentlemen and a few dowagers who were avid whist players.

And Freddie.

Max halted in mid-step, taking a second look into the room. There was no missing that turban, even though Freddie was seated all the way across the room, in front of the velvet-covered windows.

Max crossed the threshold with assumed casualness, but he could have leapt in hooting, performing a Scottish sword dance for all the attention he would have aroused. Everyone was far too intent upon their cards.

The parlor was decorated according to the Channings' passion for the classics. Max had always found the painted frescoes rather amusing, bacchanalian revelry with gentlemen in tight curls swilling down wine, leering centaurs carrying off naked maidens.

But he felt strangely uncomfortable with Freddie present, for once wishing those ladies' abundant charms were adorned with some tastefully placed flower garlands.

But Freddie seemed oblivious to her surroundings. Bent over the cards splayed in her hand, she was seated at a table with General Fortescue, Lady Diedre McCaulay, and Mr. Horace Canterfield.

Judging from the pile of coin, Fortescue appeared the big winner, a fact he did not much regard, being possessed of a large fortune. Lady McCaulay seemed a trifle put out, but it was well known that she was the Duke of Portnoy's latest mistress and he always made her losses good.

As for Canterfield, he was a hardened enough gamester merely to look bored. What he lost tonight he would attempt to recoup tomorrow at hazard or the faro table.

But Freddie . . . Max wished he could believe it was only the candlelight making her look so pale. He had seen that look of desperation too many times not to recognize it, the moisture beaded on the brow, the fretted underlip, all signs of a gamester about to be run off his, or, in this case her, pretty legs.

She was taking so long over her discard, it seemed her life depended upon it. Maybe it did.

But she was supposed to be quite wealthy, Max thought. Yet Lavinia's recent words kept echoing through his head. *Cut out of the will . . . Turned out of doors.*

Surely if she had been left penniless, the woman ought to know better than to be playing so deep. He hesitated, reminding himself it was none of his concern. For heaven's sake, the girl did not even remember who he was. But at that moment, Freddie chanced to glance up from her table and see him. Even from across the room there was no mistaking the look of mute appeal she flashed at him before bending back over her cards.

So the chit was in over her head. Max gave a faint sigh of resignation. Well, he supposed it would not take that much effort on his part to extricate her. But when he had, he would make it clear to her he was no longer in the habit of rescuing damsels in distress.

Smoothing his sleeves, he strode across the room, coming to stand just behind her chair. Freddie had folded her hand. She was signing her name to a vowel and gloomily shoving it across the table to Fortescue.

"So unfortunate, milady," the general commiserated. "But perhaps you will have better luck next hand."

"There won't be a next hand," Max said.

All heads at the table turned toward him except Freddie's.

Max summoned up a benign smile, touching her lightly on the shoulder. "You promised to dance with me this evening, Cousin Frederica, remember?"

She raised her head slowly. Max expected gratitude, at least relief. He was not at all prepared for the cool way her fine brows arched upward. "I don't recall doing anything of the kind."

"I fear you suffer from a faulty memory, milady," Max said, still smiling but now through clenched teeth.

"My memory is excellent, Mr. Warfield," she said.

Max wondered if he had been mistaken when he thought she had silently beseeched his aid. What the deuce was the matter with her—did she want to be rescued or not?

"Then damn it—er, that is, I am asking you now. Will you have the next waltz with me?"

She turned her shoulder on him, gathering up the cards to reshuffle the deck. "You can see that I am otherwise engaged. You are disrupting our game."

Max stood thunderstruck, feeling something of a fool and not much enjoying the sensation. He was uncertain what to do next, but Frederica's opponents at the table decided the issue.

"Oh, I believe I have had enough." Mr. Canterfield stifled a yawn and stood up. He held Lady McCauley's chair as she also rose.

"But—but we have only just begun," Freddie said.

Her protest went unheeded as Canterfield complained good-naturedly to the general. "I suppose we might as well all pack it in, curse you, Fortescue. The luck's been with you all evening."

Fortescue fingered the ends of mustache, preening. "Alas, I feel the luck is more with Mr. Warfield. He comes to bear off the fairest prize of all."

"No, I am not going to dance, General, I assure you," Freddie said. "Pray, let us continue—"

But Mr. Canterfield was already escorting Lady McCauley back to the ballroom and the general began scooping up his pile of coin and paper. Freddie watched with a look of sick dismay as her vowels were stuffed heedlessly into his waistcoat pocket. She bit down hard to steady her trembling underlip.

Beneath his irritation, Max could not help a stirring of unease. Curse it all! How badly dipped was the little fool?

The general shuffled to his feet, taking Freddie's hand, the old devil carrying her fingertips to his lips with one of those leering glances that made Max long to kick the backside of his breeches.

"If you will excuse me, m'dear. I must take m'leave. Promised Lady Marlborough to have a look in at her rout, though 'tis bound to be a deadly dull affair." He clapped Max jovially on the shoulder. "Enjoy your partner, Warfield. Possesses more than mere charm, you know. Such a solidly sensible sort of gel."

Max would have liked to favor him with a pithy opinion of what *he* thought of Frederica's good sense. But he contented himself with a curt bow, managing not to curl his lip with disdain as the general swaggered on his way. Freddie affected to forget that Max stood waiting behind her chair, continuing to play with the cards, shuffling them in wooden fashion. But he could tell how aware she was of his presence by the stiffness in her shoulders.

It would have served her right if he had just stalked away and left her. But even if he was a most reluctant knight errant, he could also be a stubborn one.

"I believe the orchestra has struck up the next waltz, milady." Max extended one hand to her almost in the manner of one flinging down a gauntlet.

She ignored it. "I did not come here tonight to dance, Mr. Warfield."

"No?" He plunked down into the chair the general had vacated. Her lips formed a slight pout that was soft and adorable, but the storm brewing in her eyes was pure Olympian goddess. She began to lay down the cards in a row before her, preparing for a game of solitaire. With the flush mounted high in her cheeks, her golden ringlets escaping from beneath that ridiculous turban, she looked more like a half-wild Gypsy than a dowager viscountess.

"So what are you planning to do?" Max asked. "Tell my fortune?"

"Oh, I don't need cards for that." She slammed down the king of hearts with a vengeance. "You will come to a violent end, Mr. Warfield. That is what usually befalls people who go about meddling in someone else's business."

"You intend to call me out simply because I asked you to dance?"

"You are not interested in dancing either. At least not with me. I strongly suspect you came and broke up my card game merely to ring a peal over me. So you might as well get on with it. Tell me, sir, what is your lecture to be about? My improper behavior as a recent widow, or the evils of gaming?"

"I'm not in the habit of giving lectures," Max snapped, forgetting that he had been planning to do just that.

"What a novelty. Everyone else in your family appears to do so." Freddie tossed her head, a rather too-bright sparkle in her eyes. "I received a lengthy sermon from Lady Bentley only this morning. Your sister, I believe?"

"I do my best not to acknowledge the connection, but yes, I fear she is." He added gruffly, "You should not let anything that Caroline might have said distress you."

"I didn't. She was most diverting. Lady Bentley merely hinted that it might be better for all concerned if I took myself off to Bath. She even offered me the use of her own house there. I rather think she hopes that I might drown taking the waters."

"No! Be poisoned perhaps, but not drowned."

This did not even cause her lips to twitch, but as Max recalled, it never had been easy to coax a smile from Freddie when she had determined not to do so.

"And you, Mr. Warfield—" she began.

"You used to call me Max."

She ignored the interruption. "Is that what you wanted to tell me, Mr. Warfield. That you also wish I would go away to Bath?"

Max's gaze roved over the lovely sculpted planes of her face down to the generous curve of her bosom. He started to assure her that her going away was the last thing he desired, when he brought himself up short. This was his little cousin, Freddie Jameson, after all. Damnation. He hadn't sat down to flirt with her.

"I have no opinion on the matter," he said with

a shrug. He suddenly felt as though he had gotten himself into deep waters here, no longer exactly sure what he was doing. Beyond stopping Freddie from hazarding so much at cards, he had given no thought to what else he might have to say to her.

He was not accustomed to dealing with young women. They either irritated him by blushing and stammering or attempting to play the coquette. But Frederica did neither. She treated him in that same offhand fashion she had as a little girl.

But she wasn't little anymore. That realization kept stabbing at him again and again, making him curiously awkward. To keep his eyes from straying to her more seductive curves, he focused on her hands instead. Gone were the stubby, childlike fingers, replaced by ones long and graceful.

Her game of solitaire was already going awry, and he watched as she deftly rearranged the pattern of the cards to suit herself.

"Do you always cheat?" he asked with a slight frown.

"Only myself, Mr. Warfield," she said. A flash of rare, sweet sadness appeared in her eyes, quickly shuttered away. "And so if you haven't come to lecture me or to advise me which hotel to put up at in Bath, what do you want, sir?"

"Just what I told you—to persuade you to dance with me."

"I am more interested in dining than dancing." She began to gather up the cards. "If I am going to the devil, I am determined not to do it on an empty stomach."

"And are you?"

"Am I what?"

"Going to the devil." After the barest hesitation, he demanded, "Exactly how much did you lose to Fortescue tonight?"

"Only a trifling sum of—" she began in defensive tones, then broke off, glaring at him. "Really, sir. I thought you did not mean to lecture."

He countered her complaint with another question. "Can you afford to pay this *trifling* sum, Freddie?"

She looked down the length of her nose at him. "I am accustomed to being addressed as your ladyship."

"Very well, then," he said irritably. "Can *your ladyship* afford to pay?"

She rose slowly to her feet. He could tell the gesture was meant to be one of icy dignity, but she was flushed and trembling too much. "I suppose you mean well, Mr. Warfield, but I am a woman grown and a widow. Tend to your own business and stop troubling me with—"

"Whoa! Hold up there a moment. I would never have 'troubled' you at all but for that look you shot in my direction."

"Look? What look?"

"The big blue eyes, the beseeching lips."

She looked a little flustered by the accusation, but was quick to recover herself with a shrug. "You have a fanciful imagination, sir. I—I did nothing of the kind. I don't beg. I am a lady of wealth and independence. I can wager any sum I choose and—and I am tired of being quizzed and badgered by—by a parcel of elderly, doddering relatives!"

"Elderly, doddering—" Max gasped. "Why, you little shrew!"

But before he could say anything more, she slapped down the deck of cards, then turned on her heel and flounced from the room. By the time Max had gotten to his own feet, she was well on her way out the door.

He could feel a faint hint of color in his own face

and half expected to find himself the cynosure of all eyes. But Frederica had not shouted at him. It only seemed as if she had.

None of the other whist players raised so much as an eyebrow, and Max was relieved that their avidity for cards prevented anyone from noticing that the imperturbable Mr. Warfield had just received a stinging setdown.

"Elderly, doddering relative, indeed," he muttered, Freddie's words having stung more than he cared to admit. Was that how she saw him now?

He was annoyed, but less with Freddie than himself. And Caroline. Had he not told his sister this would be the likely outcome of any effort on his part to interfere with Frederica? And knowing that, he had proceeded to do so anyway and gotten the exact response he had predicted and so richly merited.

Stupid! And most unlike himself. He was many reprehensible things, but he had always flattered himself that being an idiot did not number among them. Now he was not so sure.

You ought to know better, Warfield, he thought grimly. Never go around saving damsels until you are sure they want to be rescued. He would require the next one to submit her request for help into writing, and then he would cheerfully rip it up and settle back comfortably at his own fireside. Let some other poor sot play the hero. It was not his style.

Feeling that he had made enough of a fool of himself for one evening, Max resolved to seek out his hostess and take his leave. He would have been just as pleased not to encounter his cousin again. But having lost sight of Freddie for most of the evening, it seemed inevitable that now he would trip over her wherever he went.

He was but passing through the mahogany dining room, where an elegant buffet had been laid out on the white linen surface of a massive table. The branches of the silver candlesticks cast an inviting glow over chafing dishes filled with pastries, lobster, oyster pâtés, and steaming hot rolls.

But the chamber was as yet deserted except for the young woman with the cascade of blond curls standing at the far end of the table.

Max froze in the shadows of the doorway, watched as Freddie slipped along the length of the table, glancing nervously around her. She had removed that foolish turban and he could not but applaud the effect—that is, until he realized what she was doing. Quickly scooping something off the table, she dropped it into the depths of the turban, then balanced the headgear rather clumsily back on her head. Without a backward glance she scurried out the French doors. Like the ones from the ballroom, these also led into the garden.

Max stood, stunned for a moment until the full significance of what he had just witnessed sunk in. Freddie ... Freddie had just stolen some of the Channings' silverplate!

He had not been mistaken earlier when he had observed her play at the tables. He had guessed she might be desperate, but desperate enough to resort to thievery?

Max's lips set into a taut line. He had resolved to stay clear of the young woman, to seek no further involvement. He preferred to remain oblivious to his relatives' peccadilloes, but this was too much even for him to ignore.

Damnation, if the girl were caught at this! Likely she would not be sent to prison. The Channings would never take it that far. But the resulting scandal would ruin Frederica forever. Had she grown up to have no sense whatsoever?

Cursing Freddie for her folly and for once again forcing him to intervene, Max started after her. He bolted through the French doors, plunging into the rustling foliage of the Channings' garden for the second time that night.

The place seemed silent, a place of hushed moonlight and shadows, even the music from the ballroom at a temporary lull. Max had hoped to intercept Freddie before she scaled the wall again and reached the street, but he saw that he was already too late.

Disgruntled, he raced forward and tackled the wall himself. As he struggled for a foothold in the crumbling brick, he wondered how the deuce Freddie had cleared it, and her in skirts. Cursing at some thorny vine that snagged and tore the sleeve of his black evening coat, he managed to gain the top of the wall, marveling that Freddie could have done it so much more swiftly.

It was not until he dropped triumphantly to the other side that he realized the reason. This time she had employed the simple expediency of unlatching the garden gate and letting herself out. She was halfway up the street heading toward a coach that awaited her on the opposite corner.

Swearing, Max tore after her. His footfall must have alerted her of his approach. She cast a startled glance over her shoulder and started to run. But Max seized her by the arm and spun her around.

She shrank back, striking wildly out at him. "Let go of me or I shall scream to— Oh, it's you, Max. I—I mean Mr. Warfield." The light from the street lamp played over her delicate features. Her look of fear dissolved into one of indignation.

"You frightened me to death. Now what do you want? You cannot be this desperate for a dance partner that you need chase me through the streets."

Max paused to catch his breath. She tried to pull away, but he refused to ease his grip on her arm.

"No, I would not seem to be the one who is desperate. You little fool!" He gave her a brisk shake. "I saw you back there."

"So you did! When you were busy ruining my evening—"

"I am not talking about the cards. I realize you must be in a great deal of trouble, but there is no need for you to resort to this."

"Resort to what? So I cannot afford to own a coach and have to slip away to take a hackney. It is not against the law."

"But other things you have been doing are. Come on, Freddie. We are going to have to put it back."

"Put what back? I have no idea what you are talking about," she said loftily, but her eyes shifted, unable to meet his.

"I am talking about this." Before she could protest, he wrenched off her turban.

"Are you mad?" she spluttered. "Give me that back."

But as Max gave the garment a good shake, something wrapped in a napkin tumbled to the paving stones. He nudged the cloth with his foot, expecting to reveal the gleam of silver. Instead, a half-dozen maids of honor tumbled into the gutter, the small cakes leaving a trail of crumbs.

He blinked, then stared uncomprehending at Freddie. Shamefaced but still defiant, she cried, "Very well. I suppose you might as well have the rest of it."

Groping in the folds of skirt, she produced several more cloth bundles from concealed pockets. She thrust the parcels into his hands, a delicious spicy scent carrying to his nostrils, a splash of some rich sauce dampening his cuff.

"Lobster? Chicken aspic?" he muttered, feeling like the greatest idiot this side of Bedlam. He hardly knew what to say or do next, when a shriek rent the night air.

He heard the click of heels approaching from behind him, saw Freddie tense, her eyes widening in alarm.

"No, Dora," she called. "Stop. It is all right—"

Max had little time to make sense of these cryptic words, but enough to guess he stood in some sort of danger. He whipped around to see a large female bearing down on him, like something out of legends of the Valkyries. With his hands full of Freddie's supper, he was too slow to react. The butt end of a pistol swung out, clipping him on the side of the head.

Max reeled dizzily for a moment, then pitched to his knees, falling into the gutter as darkness claimed him.

Chapter 5

Max lay sprawled upon the red velvet chaise longue in Frederica's front parlor. Even with the combined efforts of herself, Dora, and Stubbins, that had been as far as they could get the still-unconscious Max, his hard-muscled frame weighing a good deal more than at first had appeared.

The chaise was one of the few pieces of furniture in the parlor, the elegant Grecian-style sofa having been bought in a moment of rash enthusiasm one long-ago time when Freddie had actually *won* something at lottery tickets.

Dora had had to fetch a candlestick from the dining room. She held the taper aloft with a trembling hand, its soft glow seemed to cast a harsh light upon Max's pallid features. Freddie hovered over him anxiously, applying a cold cloth to the knot upon his temple. She felt a little relieved when Max emitted a low moan.

"Thank heavens, I think he may be coming to his senses."

"Oh, dear, oh, dear," Dora said for perhaps the thousandth time since Max had first collapsed into the street. "You know I never meant to, Freddie— That is, I thought he was a footpad. I never imagined he was someone you knew. Your cousin, you say? Are you quite sure?"

"Quite sure," Freddie murmured, her gaze skating over the familiar line of rock-hard, stubborn jaw, the glossy ebony hair, the full curve of those mocking lips.

"He is called Max, after nobody in particular." A rueful half smile tipped Freddie's lips at the remembrance. For a long time in her childhood innocence she had really believed that was his surname. Max After-Nobody-in-Particular. She had thought it quite grand.

But she was quick to shrug off the memory, as she had earlier that evening when she had first suffered the shock of meeting Max again after so many years, then feigned not to know him. It had astonished her just how well she did remember him, though in her mind's eye, his features had not been cast so harsh. But her memories had been those of a child, rose-colored visions confused with notions of knights in shining armor and princes riding white chargers. She hated to think how much of her childhood she had spent with her nose pressed against the glass, waiting for this particular errant knight to come riding down the drive to rescue the princess from the ogre's castle.

But Prince Charming had never kept his promise, had never come back, and in the end the princess had had to rescue herself. Freddie thought she had put aside all recollection of Max and his defection. To admit that she still felt any hurt because of it would be the same as admitting she could be vulnerable, and she was not about to do that. She patted the compress upon his brow, her hand a little rougher than she meant it to be.

Max groaned again and flung up one arm as though to fend her off. He shifted on the chaise and moved his lips as though trying to speak, but his eyes remained closed.

"Perhaps we should fetch a doctor," Dora said.

"Where would we find a physician at this hour of night? Or pay for one if we did." Freddie frowned, lifting the cloth long enough to peer at Max's injury. The swelling had gone down considerably. "I can't understand it. The wound does not seem that great. I thought he would be roused by now."

"I did not mean to hit him so hard," Dora said.

"I am just thankful you did not shoot him."

"Oh, I couldn't have done that. I know only how to aim the pistol, not load it." Dora started to wring her hands and nearly dropped the candle, spattering hot wax everywhere.

"Take care, Dora. Let us not burn him as well," Freddie admonished. "No doubt he already will be eager to haul us up before the nearest magistrate."

"What will we do if he dies?" Dora wailed. "I shall be hung for murder."

"Nonsense. You know I should never let such a thing happen to you. I'd—I'd stuff his body up the chimney first."

"No!"

Max's sudden rebuttal was little more than a grunt, but it startled both Freddie and Dora as much as if he had bellowed.

"Not . . . chimney," he muttered, his eyes flickering at last. "Won't draw properly. Best weight me down . . . drop in Thames."

Freddie started to laugh, but her relief at this sign of his recovery was tempered with indignation. "Exactly how long have you been conscious?" she demanded. "Have you been lying there listening to us fret over you the whole time? Why didn't you say something?"

"Didn't sound to me ... as if doing much fretting. Been trying to decide if it would hurt to talk."

"And does it?" Freddie asked anxiously.

"Like hell." With an irritated motion, he brushed away both her hand and the compress. "Stop slopping water on me." He managed to shove himself up onto one elbow. "And do we need to ... have so many blasted candles."

Freddie cast one look at the single wavering taper in Dora's hand, then placed her hands gently on Max's shoulders. "I think you better lie back down."

But he resisted her, struggling to a sitting position. He blinked, seeming to focus on Dora, a dark scowl settling over his features.

"Ah, the Valkyrie."

"N-no, sir. Actually, I'm Miss Applegate, Frederica's companion." Dora dropped a nervous curtsy. "And I'm so very sorry."

"Not as sorry as I am." Max gingerly felt the lump swelling just at his hairline. He stifled a curse.

"It looks much better than when we first brought you here," Dora said. "Doesn't it, Freddie? I daresay, if he combs his hair over the other way, no one will even notice."

Max shot Dora such a black look, Freddie made haste to suggest, "Dora, dear, why don't you fetch Mr. Warfield a glass of brandy?"

Dora's eyes went around. "But Freddie, we don't have any."

Freddie groped in the concealed pocket of her gown and produced a small flask, some of the spoils she had forgotten to hand over to Max earlier.

Max's eyes narrowed. "Lord Channing's French stock. I am glad to see you at least had the wit to steal the very best."

Freddie felt her cheeks flood with color, but she compressed her lips, saying nothing. She took the candle from Dora and lit one of the tapers mounted on the wall near the fireplace, then dispatched Dora on her errand to fetch a glass. But the older woman hesitated upon the threshold, her broad, honest brow knit with concern.

"I am not sure this is proper, Frederica. Leaving you alone with a gentleman at this hour."

Freddie stifled an urge to break into hysterical laughter. Considering some of the risks she had already taken that evening, Dora's sudden concern for the proprieties was ludicrous.

Before Freddie could reassure her, Max spoke up, saying rather sourly, "There is no need to worry about me, ma'am. I'm only one of her elderly, doddering relatives."

Dora looked far from convinced, but went on her way. Freddie bit back a satisfied smile. Max Warfield always seemed so cool, if not mocking, at least aggravatingly teasing. It was good to know that she had managed to nettle him a little.

But her satisfaction was marred when she noted how pale he looked. He forced himself to stand, then reeled a little on his feet. Freddie hastened over to clutch at his arm.

"I don't think this is wise, Mr. Warfield. You should lie down. You don't look at all the thing."

But he shook her off, resisting her attempts to ease him back onto the chaise, seeking the support of the fireplace mantel instead.

Candlelight played over his drawn features as he studied his surroundings. "Where the deuce am I?"

"In my town house in Cheapside."

She thought his brows rose a little at that, and added defensively, "It may not be Grosvenor

Square, but it is still quite a respectable neighborhood."

Max paced off a few steps. Freddie watched him with bated breath, but he seemed steady enough now. He continued to inspect the chamber, his scowl deepening. Freddie had always been rather proud of her front parlor. It had the loveliest hand-painted French wallpaper, to say nothing of the elaborate carvings on the ceiling.

But Max's footsteps seemed to echo very loudly off the uncarpeted floor, the near-empty parlor smacking more of a house for let than a lived-in residence.

She should have had him laid out in the dining room. It was a little better furnished than this room with its solitary chaise, scattering of mismatched Hepplewhite chairs, and sofa tables. Before he could make any remark, Freddie summoned up a brazen smile.

"Do you like my decor, Mr. Warfield? Simplicity . . . it is all the dernier cri these days. The uncluttered look."

The door connecting to the study had been left ajar, and he stole a peek inside before remarking dryly. "How very fashionable the next room is. You have nothing at all in there."

Freddie lifted her chin. "If you came here to criticize—"

"I did not come here at all," he reminded her in rather testy accents. "You brought me."

"I suppose you would have preferred it if I had left you lying in the gutter. It would have been far simpler to have done so. Dora and I had a dreadful time getting you into the hackney. If the driver had not taken pity upon us and helped because he thought you were bosky, we never would have managed it." Freddie smiled a little. "He said, when you came round, I should give you a dreadful scold for being so ungentlemanlike as to get foxed when you were escorting ladies."

Max did not return her smile, his thick brows coming together like black thunderheads.

"I can see plainly that you have no sense of humor about this entire affair. It was all an honest mistake. Dora thought you were attacking me. But go ahead," she said, drawing herself up into a dramatic pose, holding both hands out as though waiting to be shackled. "Send for the constable. You can have me and my poor companion clapped up in Newgate before cock's crow."

"Please. Enact me no Cheltenham tragedies." He rubbed the back of his neck, wincing. "My head is already aching fit to burst."

"Then I should summon a hackney and have you taken home," she said eagerly. "Bed is what you need."

"I would be very happy to be home in my own bed, but I have a few things I need to say to you first, Frederica."

That had an ominous sound to it. She turned stubbornly away. "I cannot imagine anything so important that will not keep until—"

"Sit down, milady."

"I wonder what is keeping Dora. I should go help her to find the glasses."

"I said sit down!"

She whipped to face him, her cheeks heating. "I do not like being bellowed at."

He clutched his head. "Believe me. I am not going to bellow again. Now, please. Sit down."

She complied, sinking reluctantly onto the chaise, spreading out her skirts to conceal how ill at ease she was. He stalked over and sat down beside her, letting go his breath in a long sigh. When she had been a child, Max had always seemed quite large to her, a towering giant. She would have thought that the passage of time and her added inches would have diminished that effect.

But if anything, she had a heightened awareness of how tall and broad-shouldered he was, the way his skin-tight breeches molded the muscular outline of his thighs. Her heart set up a peculiar fluttering at his proximity. She tried to put a little more distance between them on the chaise longue, but scoot one more inch and she would end up on the floor.

Freddie expected a tongue-lashing. It had been humiliating enough, Max witnessing her losses at the card table, but then to also catch her behaving like a pickpocket, pilfering food from the Channings' buffet! She had to fight down the urge to blush with shame. Max would likely have quite a few caustic remarks to make about her behavior. He had a very cutting wit, and being coshed over the head was bound to render any man a little surly. Freddie braced herself for the worst.

She was a good deal surprised when his hand reached out to cover her own, his callused palm chafing her skin. Her gaze flew to his face. He looked quite disreputable, dark strands of hair tumbled across his brow, the spectacular bruise upon his forehead, his cravat disheveled, the very picture of a rakehell after a wild night on the town.

But his gray eyes were somber, his expression grave as he asked, "Freddie, how long have you been going on this way?"

She moistened her lips, and said brightly, "Goodness, I don't know what you mean, Mr. Warfield. What way?"

He indicated the room with an expressive frown.

"Living so—so uncluttered. Do you even have any servants?"

"Yes! I have a very fine butler and a housemaid, which quite suffices for my needs. There is not much to dust."

"Just how badly off did your late husband leave you?"

"Merely because I choose to live simply is no reason for you to assume—"

"Cut line, Freddie. You know I can always find out the terms of the viscount's will just by checking with the family solicitors."

She withdrew her hand from his grasp. Freddie struggled a moment more with her pride before replying. "Very well, if you insist upon prying into my affairs, sir, I will tell you . . . I was left practically penniless and soon after the funeral, my stepson turned me out of doors."

"That bastard!"

"Yes," Freddie agreed. "That is a very accurate summary of Sir Wilfred's character."

"I was not speaking of Sir Wilfred, but your late husband."

"I beg your pardon," Freddie said, stiffening.

Max was treading upon dangerous ground, but appeared quite unaware of it. "That old bounder! To wed an innocent young girl, then leave her unprovided for! How the Jamesons could have forced you to wed a demi-rep with one foot in the grave—"

"Mr. Warfield." Her hands knotted into fists. "If you want to keep all your teeth, I strongly advise you not to say anything more about Leon."

"Leon?"

"Lord Raincliffe." She felt a hot stinging behind her eyes and blinked furiously. "He—he was magnificent, and I won't let anyone abuse his memory. Not even you."

He regarded her with a puzzled frown, then re-marked slowly, "I am sorry if I said anything to distress you. Apparently I misunderstood about your marriage. I spoke only out of concern for you. How do you contrive to live?"

"I manage well enough," she snapped.

"Were tonight's activities supposed to be a sam-ple of that? Wandering the streets alone, losing large sums at cards, being obliged to steal your sup-per?"

"I took only what I would have eaten if I had stayed to dine."

"Or if you had been a starving waif who had not had a decent meal for several days."

Freddie glared at him. "Well, I had Dora to think of, too, didn't I?"

He shoved abruptly to his feet, like a man who has reached some resolution, one he found unpleas-ant. He started to rake his hand back through his hair, but winced, checking the motion. Pacing back toward the fireplace, he said, "Much as I hate to admit it, my sister Caroline was right."

"Right about what?" Freddie asked suspiciously.

"Something has to be done about you before you break your neck scaling walls, get arrested for theft, or assault some other helpless fellow whose head may not be as hard as mine. You are badly in need of a strong hand at the reins, my girl."

"Indeed, Mr. Warfield. And just whose strong hand did you have in mind?"

"Little as I relish the prospect, the task seems to have fallen to me." He gave vent to a weary sigh. "To begin with, I shall, of course, have to pay your gaming debts with the understanding that I will not see you with a deck of cards in your hands again. Then the lease on this house will have to be given up. Temporarily, you will have to move in with one of my sisters."

Freddie shot to her feet, outrage rendering her momentarily speechless.

"Most likely it should be Lady Bentley," he continued. "It would serve Caroline right for attempting to drag me into this business to begin with."

"Mr. Warfield!" Freddie gasped, finding her voice at last. He regarded her with unraised eyebrows, as though surprised that she should have anything to say in the matter, a fact that only added fuel to her mounting anger.

"How dare you!" she spluttered. "What makes you think that after all these years I will permit you to charge back into my life again and start ordering me around? You always were infernally high-handed."

"Always?" Beneath his heavy lids, those keen gray eyes seemed to bore into her. "I thought you said you did not remember me."

Freddie started guiltily, then made haste to recover her error. "I—I don't. I meant that—that you were high-handed tonight, the way you interrupted my card game, persisted in following me, and now this. Standing there calmly planning my future. I cannot even think why you would trouble yourself. I doubt that you suffer much from any great sense of family duty."

"I don't."

"Then why come bothering me?"

He gave a careless shrug. "Call it a whim, if you like. I must be growing sentimental in my dotage. You still remind me so much of that wayward little girl I once knew."

"Perhaps you should take a closer look," she said tartly.

"Oh, I already have," he murmured. He stepped

toward her, and Freddie experienced a sudden wild impulse to retreat. But she stood her ground as his lean, strong fingers cupped her chin, tilting her face up to the light. He subjected her to a lingering inspection that caused the blood to fire into her cheeks.

Leon had often done the same, teasingly catching her chin when he wanted to be assured of her full attention. But Leon's touch, she was forced to admit, had never sent her heart pounding so madly.

She wanted to draw away, but found herself strangely unable to stir. She returned Max's gaze as though mesmerized, her eyes drawn to the full shape of his mouth. He was smiling slightly, the movement of his lips so enticing, it took her a moment before she could concentrate upon what he was saying.

". . . and you have grown to be a beautiful woman."

She wanted to tell him she did not care for his compliments, but she was surprised to discover she did. She blushed like any simpering debutante, stammering, "Th-thank you."

"A pity you have not acquired some wisdom to match that lovely profile." He gave her chin one final playful flick.

The dismissive gesture as much as the mockery of his words restored Freddie to her senses. She stepped back from him and grated, "I am wise enough to know one thing, sir. That I will live as I choose with no help or hindrance. And if you think otherwise, you may go and be damned."

"Likely I will," he drawled. "But first I intend to make sure you don't follow suit."

Although amusement glimmered in his smoke gray eyes, his jaw set in a manner that matched her own stubborn resolve, and Freddie regretted that she had never been able to afford any china to adorn her mantel. She longed for something to throw at him, a plate, a vase. It didn't even have to be Sèvres.

It was at that moment that Dora rustled back into the room, bearing a tray and glasses. She beamed at both of them, as ever oblivious to any undercurrents of tension.

"Oh, Mr. Warfield," she trilled. " 'Tis such a relief to see you on your feet again. And the color back in your face, too. I am sorry I took so long. I had difficulty finding any clean glasses. Poor Till has been so busy with the baby, and when Stubbins does the washing up— Well, you know what his eyes are!"

Max didn't, and Freddie was not keen to have him enlightened any further about her unorthodox domestic arrangements.

"I am sorry you were put to such bother, Dora," Freddie said. "Mr. Warfield was just on the point of leaving.

"And he will not be coming back," she added, low enough that only he could hear.

"At least not tonight," he murmured.

Looking crestfallen, Dora set the tray down upon the sofa table. "But—but, oh, dear. Do you really feel well enough to go, sir? If you should collapse again . . . I feel so responsible. You will never forgive me."

"On the contrary, madam. There is nothing to forgive." Max strode over and took Dora's hand, the offhand kiss he brushed on her fingertips nonetheless leaving the elderly spinster blushing and flustered. "Take care of my wayward cousin until I return. She seems to need a great deal of looking after."

"Oh, I am. I—I mean I shall."

"Good-bye, Mr. Warfield," Freddie said point-edly.

"Au revoir, my dear." Max gave her one of his infuriatingly languid grins. "Don't bother to ring for the butler. I can find my own way out."

"A good thing, too," Dora said. "For I doubt if Stubbins could."

Luckily Max was already slipping out the door and he did not seem to hear this frank if imprudent remark. The door was left ajar and Freddie rushed across the room and slammed it closed as though she would bar it against Max's threatened return.

Dora sighed. "Such an abrupt man, your cousin. He is not at all handsome, but likely he looks better when he has not been hit over the head." She added wistfully, "I hope he does come back. It would be so pleasant to have a gentleman calling upon us. I could act as chaperone and pour out the tea."

"If Mr. Warfield calls upon us again, we are not going to be at home."

"Why, Freddie." Dora regarded her with a mixture of mild reproach and surprise.

"Don't you understand?" Freddie asked impatiently. "He is as bad as any of my other cousins, as bad as Lady Bentley or Aunt Jameson, scheming for a way to be rid of me. You should have heard him before you came back into the room, calling me a nuisance, saying how he would have this house closed up, send me to live with his sisters."

Dora went quite pale, her lower lip trembling. "That means I should have to return to Dorchester, to live with Wilfred and his family."

"No, it doesn't. For I won't let it happen. I shall send Mr. Max Warfield to the right just as I have all the others. We want none of his meddling."

"No." Dora gave her a wobbly smile. "And I am

sure with all you won tonight, we will be able to snap our fingers at the entire world."

Freddie found herself unable to meet Dora's hopeful gaze.

"You—you did win, didn't you, Freddie?"

"No, Dora. I didn't. I fear I lost quite a dreadful sum."

She sank down upon the chaise while Dora swallowed hard with disappointment, then tried to put a brave front upon it.

"Oh, well. I am sure you will win next time."

Freddie only shook her head. "I am beginning to realize I am not cut out to make my living as a gamester. I always thought I was so brilliant at cards. I fear all those times Leon must have been letting me win."

She propped her elbows on her knees, allowing her chin to droop upon her hands. "The truth is, Dora, I don't quite know what we are going to do."

It had been a total disaster of a night, between her losses at the tables and that humiliating episode that had resulted in Max Warfield's intrusion back into her life. What else could possibly go wrong?

It was a question that unfortunately was answered the next morning. Despite her pressing worries, Freddie had been exhausted enough to sleep soundly. She had roused herself, slipped into a morning frock of sprigged muslin, and was in the process of arranging her hair beneath a lacy cap when Till barged into the room.

"Oh, madam, you must come at once." The winsome housemaid gasped. "There must be some great trouble. Stubbins is at the front door, arguing and trying to bar admittance to somebody."

"Another bill collector!" Freddie groaned. Could they not even have the decency to wait until after breakfast. She was tempted to dive back beneath the covers and pull them over her head.

But she could not leave poor Stubbins in the lurch, manfully but singlehandedly attempting to guard the castle. The erstwhile coachman was far more accustomed to dealing with recalcitrant horses than people.

Her hair tumbling in a golden sheen around her shoulders, her lace cap still askew, Freddie bolted from her room. She was nearly all the way down the stairs leading to the front hall when she paused.

For the first time, it occurred to her, it might not be a bill collector at all, but Max making good on his threat to return. Freddie raised one hand and started to self-consciously smooth back the wild disarray of her tresses. She stopped almost at once, angry with herself. What did she care what Max Warfield might think about her appearance?

As she hesitated on the last step, she could see the agitated Stubbins attempting to close the front door. He said in querulous tones, "You must come back later. Her ladyship is not even out of bed yet."

"Stubbins?" Freddie called out.

"Eh?" The old man whirled around, squinting in her direction. "That be you, milady? Beggin' yer pardon. Did not mean to rouse you with this fracas."

"Who is out there?"

"Hanged if I can be sure, milady. Can't get any sense out of the fellow. Says his name is Wilfred Raincliffe."

Frederica paled. "Wilfred! Here?"

"I didn't say any such thing, you old fool," an impatient young voice piped up. "Let me pass."

The next instant, the door was shoved wider, and a short, stout boy of about ten dodged past Stubbins and into the hallway. He appeared a sturdy lad with ruddy cheeks and a shock of sun-streaked blond hair. He was attired in tan trousers and a navy blue short jacket, and his apparel looked dusty from traveling.

Spying Freddie, he made her a magnificent leg which was all that was elegant and polite, but the devil fair danced in his sparkling blue eyes.

"Your servant, milady," he said grandly, sweeping a soft-brimmed cap from his waving locks.

Astonishment warred with amusement in Freddie at such a courtly display from so youthful a gallant.

"Sir," she said, biting back a smile, managing to curtsy with perfect gravity. "What means this intrusion? What sort of tale have you been foisting off upon my butler about being Sir Wilfred?"

"Faith, milady," he trilled. "Your pardon, but I told the muttonhead no such thing. I said Lord Wilfred Raincliffe was my father."

"Your f-father?" Freddie faltered.

"Indeed. I am St. John Bartholmy Barry." The sunny features darkened for a moment. "B'God, did you ever hear anything so awful. I prefer to be called Jack."

"How do you do, Master Jack," Freddie said, her mind whirling. Of course she knew of the existence of Sir Wilfred's children. But during the entire course of her marriage, her stepson had never suffered her to meet any of his offspring. It made no sense that with Leon gone and Sir Wilfred well rid of her, the dour man would now choose to relent.

Thoroughly bewildered, Freddie let her gaze flutter toward the door Stubbins had closed with a disgruntled shake of his head. She feared to see Wilfred come striding in, his long nose twitching as ever with disapproval.

She glanced back to the boy, asking doubtfully, "Your papa brought you here to call upon me?"

" 'Course not, milady. Have you maggots 'neath your cap? I am supposed to be at school."

"Then—then what—"

"I ran away." He gave her an engaging grin. "To you. You are my *grandmama*, are you not?"

Chapter 6

Freddie sank into a chair behind the pine work-table in the kitchen, feeling she had of a sudden aged considerably beyond her twenty-one years. Perhaps the acquisition of a grandson did that to one, she thought with a wry smile. She stared in bemusement at the boy seated opposite her, licking a drip of honey from his fingers with great relish. Master Jack had already devoured half a loaf of bread and now darted eager glances to where Till stirred a pot of porridge over the open range, all the while rocking her baby's cradle with her foot.

Freddie had not so much as touched her own steaming cup of chocolate. She was still reeling with the shock of the child's announcement. Her first impulse was to discredit it entirely. How could a lively imp with such an engaging smile have ever sprung from Sir Wilfred's scrawny loins? And yet when St. John looked up at her, those devils dancing in those vivid blue eyes, there was something sweetly familiar about him that brought a lump to her throat.

No, not so much Sir Wilfred's son, but very much Leon's grandchild.

Freddie swallowed thickly and glanced quickly away to hide her tears. She had a notion that young

Master Jack would not take too kindly to being wept over.

But she soon discovered that she had not entirely given the lad his due. Along with that spark of mischief, he appeared to have inherited his grandfather's innate sense of chivalry. Moments later when Dora skittered into the kitchen, having heard of the boy's arrival, she swept him into her arms, tears pouring down her cheeks.

Jack bore it stoically, merely crinkling his snub nose and murmuring, " 'Faith, lady, have a little mercy on all that remains of a fellow's best shirt-front."

"Oh, Master St. John. I—I never thought to see you again," Dora sobbed. "How—how you have grown."

"I don't see why that should make you cry," Jack said with frank bewilderment. "I could not help it."

This only provoked Dora into a fresh spasm of sentimental tears and several more hugs until Freddie thought it time to rescue the poor lad. Dora was full of questions regarding Jack's sudden appearance on their doorstep, but Freddie refused to allow the child to be badgered until his appetite had been appeased.

Two bowls full of porridge later, he settled back in his chair with a satisfied sigh. Rather hopefully he requested a mug of ale to wash it all down, but settled for a glass of milk.

After a long draft at his glass, he emerged with a milky mustache that was all boy, but the tidy way he applied his napkin would have done justice to the most elegant courtier.

Freddie said gravely, "And now, Master Jack, perhaps you would be so good as to explain what brought you here."

"Why, the stage, madam," he said, the wide blue

eyes much too innocent. "Lots of fellows travel that way."

"That is not what I meant, as you perfectly well know, sir. I want to know what induced you to run away, come to London in this fashion."

"Oh, I had been planning this for some time. Of course I would have come much sooner if I had realized what a fetching grandmama I have."

Dora gasped at this piece of audaciousness. Jack regarded Freddie through the thickness of his lashes, shooting her the most heart-melting grin. What a charming devil he was already. Give him ten more years and— Freddie suppressed the amused thought behind a quelling frown.

When she sternly demanded that he stop offering her Spanish coin and proceed with his explanation, Jack became more subdued, though there was no way to entirely douse the twinkle in those blue eyes.

"I had simply had enough of school," he said indignantly. " 'Tis not even a good school like Eton, where a fellow could learn something important like cricket. Nay, 'tis all Latin and Greek, from morn till night, until a man's brain is fit to burst. But then, Cliveden gave me the happy notion of running off to London."

"Cliveden?" Freddie asked.

"Sir Wilfred's oldest son," Dora explained. "He must be nearly sixteen by now."

"Seventeen," Jack added gloomily.

"And the very image of Sir Wilfred."

Freddie grimaced. As far as she was concerned, Dora did not describe Sir Wilfred's heir any further. The name Cliveden alone was enough to conjure up a most unwelcome vision.

"If your brother is so much like your papa," Freddie told Jack, "I cannot imagine this Cliveden suggesting you do anything so audacious as run away."

"That slow-top. 'Course he didn't. But he *inspired* me." Jack's broad grin faded. "Clive sometimes visits me at school. Oh, not like the other fellows' big brothers who come to slip one a guinea or take one out for a ride. No, Clive comes only to prose at me or to find out what mischief I have been about so that he can squeak beef to Papa.

"The last time Cliveden came"—Jack paused, a slight quiver in his voice—"it was to bring me black armbands because of—of Grandpapa dying and all."

The child's grief-stricken expression matched the sense of loss Freddie still so often felt. She could not resist reaching across the table to squeeze his hand. Although Jack looked embarrassed, he made no movement to draw away.

Swallowing hard, he continued. "Cliveden was so smug, telling me what had happened after the funeral, how you had just been sent away. It was the shabbiest thing I had ever heard of. I decided that very day to come to London as soon as I could to visit you."

Jack went on to describe how he had attempted to save coach fare from his miserly allowance. After months of failing in that, he had formed a new plan. He had faked illness to be confined to his bed, then slipped away, managing to sell his watch, then catch the stage.

"But however did you find us?" Dora asked, obviously as enthralled at hearing the tale of this daring escapade as Jack was to be telling it.

Jack sat up straighter, swaggering a little. "That was easy. I simply made the rounds of all the fashionable shops where they sell fripperies for ladies until I found one that had heard of the Dowager

Viscountess of Raincliffe and was able to give me your address."

"How did you persuade the clerk to tell you—" Freddie began, took one look into those outrageous blue eyes, and stopped. "Never mind," she muttered. "Foolish question."

"Oh, how very brave and enterprising you are," Dora cooed.

Recalling what courage and resource it had taken to get herself to London, Freddie was inclined to agree. But she held her tongue. The boy was becoming puffed up enough with Dora's admiration.

"Aye." Jack gloated, looking well pleased with himself. "It was clever of me, wasn't it? Perhaps I shall become a Bow Street Runner when I am grown."

"Yes, er—that is all very well, Master Jack," Freddie interrupted at last. "But one thing still puzzles me. Why did you decide to come to me? You had never even met me."

"No-ooo," he said. "But if Cliveden and my papa said you were such a horrid person, I was certain you had to be wonderful. I thought we could have the most bang-up holiday together. We could go see the Royal Menagerie and Astley's Amphitheatre, have ices at Gunther's and—"

"That would be lovely," Dora cried.

"Dora!" Freddie shot her a repressive frown. Young Jack needed no further encouragement in this folly. Freddie saw that it was her unhappy lot to point out to the boy how reckless his actions had been. When she thought of the things that might have befallen a young boy traveling alone, wandering the streets of London, it was enough to chill her blood.

"Jack," she began gently, "I am quite delighted to make your acquaintance at last, but you must see that you have behaved very badly. Your mama and papa will be quite worried when they find you have gone—"

"No one will even notice," Jack interrupted with a rebellious sniff.

"Of course they will. If you wanted to come to London, the proper thing to have done—" Freddie paused, wincing a little at her own tone. She was beginning to sound like someone's maiden aunt. How dreadful. But she continued doggedly. "The proper thing would have been to ask your papa to bring you to the city."

"He wouldn't. I never have holidays, not like all the other fellows. Biddington's uncle took him to the races at Newmarket once and Stokely went to the seaside. And at least most of the boys get to go home once in a while."

"You—you don't get to go home?" Freddie faltered.

"Papa says it is better for me to stay at school and have extra lessons."

"Oh, you poor boy," Dora cried, close to tears again.

Jack shrugged, his display of defiance doing little to conceal the wistfulness in his eyes. "Oh, I don't mind so much. I am far too old to be missing my mama or anything like that. But every fellow needs a holiday once in a while."

He angled a beguiling glance at Freddie. "We could have such a splendid time together, and you could tell me all about my grandpapa. I don't really remember him, you see. Is it true that he once fought a duel?"

"Yes, I believe that he did—"

"Good. You can tell me all about it while we are off visiting the Tower."

Freddie took one look at his smile, so bright with hope, and struggled to steel herself against it.

"I am afraid that is impossible, Jack. You cannot stay here."

"Oh, Freddie, no," Dora said.

But Freddie ignored this outcry. It was far harder to ignore the way the child's face fell.

"Sir Wilfred . . . your papa would be furious if he ever learned you had come to me," she said. "Goodness knows what he might do. I am sorry, Jack, but you will have to go back to school."

An awful silence descended upon the room after her announcement. Freddie braced herself for a barrage of pleading, perhaps even tears. But although the boy's lip trembled, he rose to his feet with great dignity.

"I understand perfectly, milady," he said in a small voice. "Of course, I have no wish to get you into any trouble. Thank you for a fine breakfast. I'll just be on my way."

Freddie suppressed a sigh, feeling like the greatest beast in nature. But she needed no more trouble laid at her door. She would escort him to the stage herself and see that he got on it. It was all for the best.

The forlorn figure retrieved his hat and shuffled past her, his shoulders bent. "I suppose I shall never see London, now. I shall likely be caned and locked into a closet until I am twenty-one. 'Course, you must not worry about me," he proclaimed in accents that would have done credit to Edmund Kean.

These melodramatic pronouncements were enough to send Dora diving for her handkerchief, but Freddie remained proof against them. Yet she could not help but be touched by the way he strove to take his disappointment like a man, the attitude at odds with the still-babelike softness of his cheeks. What proved her final undoing was the very real misery in the boy's eyes as he sketched her the most heroic little bow.

She sighed, saying gruffly, "Don't be a wet goose, Master Jack. Of course I did not mean for you to leave immediately. You must be tired from your journey. You will need to rest up a bit."

"A bit?" Jack's head came up sharply, as though he could scent her resolve weakening.

"At least for a day?" Dora said pleadingly.

"Or several days perhaps?" Jack cried. "I am *really* tired."

Freddie made one more futile struggle with her common sense. But at his appealing glance, she could do no other than nod. She said, "But then I absolutely will have to find some way to get you safely back to school."

But in the midst of the exuberant hugs she received from both Dora and Jack, Freddie was not certain that anyone was listening to her.

By the time she had dispatched Till to show the boy abovestairs, where he might wash up and rest, Freddie was berating herself for her folly. As if her life were not already on the brink of ruin, what must she do but assume responsibility for a child, a boy, moreover, with an appetite hearty enough to eat the pantry barer than it was now?

And God help her if Sir Wilfred ever found out she had housed his son, even briefly. He might have her arrested for abduction. Well, Freddie thought wearily, Newgate clearly seemed destined to be her fate. That is, if Bedlam did not claim her first.

Dora, as ever oblivious to the prospects of fresh disaster hanging over their heads, followed Freddie cheerfully as she returned to her bedchamber to finish her interrupted toilette.

"Dear little St. John," Dora chattered on. "Only fancy. I had not seen him since he was in leading strings. He has grown up so delightfully. Oh, I do wish that we might keep him."

"He is not a stray puppy, Dora," Freddie said irritably. She wished the woman would leave her alone for a while. She badly needed time to think. But Dora showed no signs of leaving, plunking down to sit upon the edge of Freddie's bed while Freddie removed her lace cap and finished the task of brushing out her hair.

She continued to lecture Dora, thinking it best to disabuse the woman of any foolish notion that Jack might ever become a permanent guest.

"He must be sent back as soon as I can arrange it. Even someone as cold-blooded as Sir Wilfred will be bound to feel anxiety at the disappearance of his son."

"Anxiety indeed!" Dora said hotly. "You heard how he abandoned the poor child at that horrid school. It affected you as well. I could tell."

Freddie paused in the act of dragging her brush through a particularly stubborn knot. She stared into the mirror and saw her own troubled eyes gaze back at her. "I fear I was thinking more of Leon," she said. "What delight he would have taken in young Jack. It—it was my fault Leon never got to know his own grandson. If Wilfred had not detested me so—" Her image shimmered before a gathering of crystal tears. Freddie bowed her head.

"Oh, no, my dear, pray don't." Dora leapt up from the bed, seeking to comfort her with little distracted gestures, patting her awkwardly upon the back. "You are not to be thinking such things. My lord and Cousin Wilfred were at odds long before Lord Raincliffe ever married you. You are not in the least to blame for the fact that horrid Wilfred never brought his children to wait upon their grandfather."

Freddie drew forth a handkerchief and mopped at her eyes, ashamed of her momentary weakness. She said briskly, "In any case, it is far too late now for any regrets. I must think about the present. Much as I loathe the notion, I will have to dispatch a note to Wilfred, assure him the boy is safe."

"Perhaps he will be so angry with Jack, he will say that we may keep him."

Freddie shot Dora a look expressive of what she thought of the absurdity of that notion. "I don't know how I would keep Jack, or anyone else for that matter."

Master Jack's unexpected arrival had been a momentary diversion, distracting Freddie from her more pressing problems—the enormous gaming debt to the general, how she would stave off the creditors who would inevitably come knocking, how she was even going to order up tonight's dinner, especially when she now had a new mouth to feed, a ten-year-old boy with a lusty appetite.

When she expressed this concern aloud to Dora, the woman frowned a moment, then said, "You have been invited to another party tonight. I can get your turban ready, cleaned up as good as new. I only hope Mr. Warfield will not be present this time to spoil things."

"Whether Max is present or not, I fear the turban will no longer answer," Freddie said with a tired smile. "I needs must find a more permanent solution."

"Permanent? What do you mean, Freddie?"

Freddie was not precisely sure herself. "I only know we cannot continue on as we have been. I suppose I am going to have to seek out some sort of a position."

"A position!" Dora was aghast. "Do you mean like—like a cook or a lady's maid."

"Or a governess."

"Perhaps I could get hired on as someone's companion," Dora suggested timidly, "but Freddie, my dear, I fear that no one would ever engage you as a governess."

Gazing at her reflection in the mirror, Freddie was bound to concede that Dora was right. With her golden hair tumbling about her shoulders, she looked absurdly youthful, a chit straight out of the schoolroom.

"I should not care for being a governess, anyway," Freddie conceded with a toss of her head. She reached behind her to squeeze Dora's hand. "Nor will I have you hiring out to be a slave to some horrid old woman. No, that is all too drearily respectable for us. We must think of something more daring."

"The stage?" Dora proposed dubiously.

The idea had a momentary appeal for Freddie, but she shook her head. "Even if I could be engaged as an actress, I don't know if I should make enough money at it to pay the staggering sum I so stupidly lost last night."

She added in disgruntled accents, "Of course, it was nothing compared to what Lady Deidre McCaulay dropped at the table, and she never turned a hair. It must be a fine thing to have a rich duke in one's pocket. Perhaps I should acquire myself a wealthy protector."

Freddie spoke only in jest. She was astonished when Dora paled, apparently taking her quite seriously.

"Oh, no. That would be a little too wicked, Freddie. And after all, you are a grandmother now."

"Only temporarily."

"And besides, your cousin Max would never permit it. He struck me as being a most forceful man. I don't believe he would at all like your becoming someone—someone's protected person."

"It would be none of Max's business," Freddie said.

"I fear he would make it so. Recollect, he did promise to call upon you again soon and he said you were to stay out of mischief until then."

"Max Warfield's promises are not always to be trusted," Freddie said bitterly. "And as for Mr. Warfield *presuming* to give me orders—" She broke off, flushing, an evil demon seeming to stir within her breast. "You truly think Max would mind my seeking a wealthy lover?"

"Most definitely," came Dora's emphatic reply.

Freddie's lips parted into a slow, hard smile. "Well, I find it an excellent notion. I wonder that I did not think of it sooner. Such an arrangement can even be respectable if managed discreetly. Lady Deidre is still received everywhere although it is well known she is the duke's mistress. She rides in an elegant carriage, drips with jewels, and has a wealthy man dancing attendance upon her every whim. What more could one want?"

"I don't know," Dora said, fretting her lower lip. "To be loved—loved *honestly* perhaps? Surely you could always marry again. You have acquired so many admirers. Young Mr. Whitby, Lord Fremont, Mr. Burke . . ."

"Fortune hunters! I doubt any of them would be so enamored of me if they realized how poor I was."

"Your lack of dowry never bothered Cousin Leon."

"Ah, but there will never be another Leon," Freddie said sadly. "No other man could be so generous, so understanding, so—" She swallowed, then firmly shook her head. "No, Dora, I am not at all interested in marrying again."

"But yet you would engage in an illicit liaison with some—some . . . oh, Freddie, my dear. Do but think. Could you truly be happy under such circumstances?"

"Why not? The wickedest people always seem to be the most happy. I have quite decided, Dora. Find me a wealthy rake and our problems will all be solved."

Dora said nothing, but her eyes spoke volumes. Freddie was accustomed to seeing nothing but unqualified admiration on the woman's plain, open features. Dora's troubled gaze unnerved her. Perhaps she had gone too far this time. She was not sure herself what she really meant by all this wild talk. She knew only that she felt more weary and frightened than she ever had in her life, completely at wit's end.

Unable to bear any more of Dora's disapproving expression, Freddie glanced away. "I did warn you not to come with me, didn't I? That I meant to lead a life of mad debauchery? If—if you chose to write Sir Wilfred and ask him if you can return with Jack, I would quite understand."

Freddie waited, for what she scarce knew, perhaps for Dora's usual reassurances. She was stunned when none came. In subdued tones, Dora merely asked to borrow some of her scented paper.

" 'Tis there, beneath the lid of my writing desk," Freddie said.

Frowning, Dora located the vellum and bustled out of the room, leaving Freddie feeling strangely bereft. So she had finally succeeded in disgusting and shocking even her devoted Dora.

She tried to shrug. Perhaps it was right for Dora to go, even for the best. The sort of mad, uncertain life Freddie proposed to lead, *was* leading, had never been right for an elderly spinster. Yet until this moment Freddie had not been aware how much she had come to depend upon Dora's loyalty and devotion.

It seemed to be her fate in life to always lose the people she came to care about. Perhaps the trick was to stop caring. Bleakly, Freddie turned back to the mirror to finish arranging her hair into a smooth topknot of curls. She was usually so clever at such things, but this morning her fingers were quite clumsy.

She had barely finished the task when Dora returned as unceremoniously as she had left. She looked more composed although her brow was furrowed in concentration. She approached Freddie, holding out a sheet of paper that Freddie could see was covered with Dora's neat, slightly crabbed handwriting.

Freddie's heart sank, but she rallied, saying with forced lightness, "Goodness! Finished so soon? I hope you set aside your pride enough to insist that Wilfred send the carriage for you or at least coach fare."

Dora regarded her blankly. "Wilfred? What has this to do with him?"

"I assume that letter is for him. . . ."

"Certainly not. Whatever would I be writing him for? This is our list."

"List? List of what?"

"Why, of all the most eligible rakes in London. If you are determined upon this course, I thought we should go about it properly." Dora beamed proudly. "A capital notion, is it not? I have grown to be so sensible and efficient since we have moved to London."

Freddie stared at her a moment. Then tears

misted her eyes. She thoroughly confounded Dora by seizing the older woman in a strong, fierce hug.

Dora gasped in astonishment. "My—my dear, Freddie. What is all this?"

"Nothing." Freddie sniffed. "Only I do not think I fully appreciated you until this moment, my very dear friend."

Dora looked equal parts flustered and pleased, as she always was by any compliment. "Well!" she said. "I did not realize I had been that clever."

"It has nothing to do with— 'Tis only that I thought—" Freddie hesitated with a shaky laugh. "Never mind. Sometimes I am a great fool. Come, show me your list."

Dora regarded her anxiously several moments longer as she feared Freddie might be losing her reason. But pride won out and she presented her paper to Freddie with a grand flourish.

The heading at the top of the page read: A Compilation of the Most Eligible and Wealthy Rakes in London.

The very notion of such a thing tickled Freddie's sense of the ridiculous, but Dora looked as solemn as a member of Parliament presenting a new bill. With a valiant struggle, Freddie composed her features not to laugh.

Peering over Freddie's shoulder, Dora pointed to the first name on the list. "Now, there is Sir Alston Walcott. Very handsome and well set up. But there is a nasty rumor about that he suffers from the pox.

"Next I listed General Fortescue. He is a little— ah, mature, but extremely well heeled. And after all, you are already in debt to him. But he does take snuff, a most disagreeable habit. Then there is Mr. Petries. He prefers dark-haired opera dancers, but you are so lovely, he might make an exception. However, he is reputed to snore loudly in bed."

Freddie no longer felt any desire to laugh. She could only stare at her friend in complete astonishment. "Dora, where in heaven's name did you ever come by such information?"

"Oh, from the housekeeper two doors down, the seamstress who does your clothes, the milliner who sold you that darling hat." Dora preened herself a little. "If I ever possessed any talent, it is for gleaning gossip. And it is all so much more interesting here in London than it ever was buried in Dunhaven."

Freddie could only shake her head. She was constantly underestimating Miss Dora Applegate. She tried to concentrate on the names that Dora continued to rattle off, the attributes and failings of the various gentlemen.

But to her dismay, she experienced a strange and uncomfortable fluttering in the pit of her stomach. It had been one thing to indulge in such bold talk of finding herself a wealthy rake. Dora's earnest concentration and her list were all making it seem somehow nerve-rackingly real.

Freddie was not quite so naive that she did not realize there was a little more to becoming a man's mistress than accepting his admiration and expensive presents. Rakehells were noted for expecting something more in return than a lady's smile.

Leon had never been able to teach her anything of a man's physical needs, but Freddie bore a vague and discomfiting notion of what would be required of her. She could already feel a knot of tension forming in her chest, but resolutely she sought to ignore it.

She was familiar, at least by sight, with most of the gentlemen Dora listed. But the thought of any of these men caressing her in intimate fashion left her feeling cold, her palms clammy.

Paying no heed to Dora's reading or comments, Freddie scanned ahead, hoping to find the mention of at least one whose touch she might be able to tolerate. She neared the bottom of the list when she drew up short.

"Dora! You have my cousin's name listed!"

"What? Oh, you mean Mr. Warfield? Well, you did say he was only a very distant relative. And he is perhaps the most eligible rake in all of London."

"Is he indeed?" Freddie asked, even the sight of Max's name enough to bring heat flaring into her cheeks, whether through anger or some other reason, she could not be sure.

"Oh, yes! They are laying bets at White's this very minute as to who his next mistress will be."

Freddie crinkled her nose in distaste. "How vulgar and crude men can be."

"Distressingly so. I did hesitate to list Mr. Warfield. The competition for his favor seems to be great. Although he did show much interest in you last night, it seemed so—so avuncular."

Freddie nearly choked. "He said I had grown to be beautiful. He—" But she broke off in mortification, remembering that Max had also said she still reminded him of a little girl.

"Truly," Dora said. "I can see I have distressed you. I don't know what I was thinking of. Indeed, I am certain he would be as horrified at the notion as you."

"Horrified?" Freddie repeated. "Yes, I suppose Max would be." She thought of Max's arrogance, how after years of neglect he had barged back into her life, lectured her as though she were still a child, the bored way he had declared it his duty to make "arrangements" for her. If the man was so determined to come to her aid, perhaps it was time to show him she had a few notions of her own, show him beyond all doubt what sort of woman she had grown to be and pay off an old score at the same time. By the time she had done with Mr. Max Warfield, she doubted he would ever seek to interfere with her again.

Despite the fire that now seemed to be racing through Freddie's veins as well as flooding her cheeks, a taut smile curved her lips.

Dora greeted Freddie's long silence with increasing nervousness. "Perhaps I had just better mark Mr. Warfield off the list." Dora extended her hand to take the paper, but Freddie held it out of her reach.

"Don't be so hasty, Dora," Freddie purred. "I think you may have had an excellent idea. In fact, if Max is so sought after, I should not leave the matter to chance. I should call on him as soon as possible."

Dora made a faint sound of protest, but as usual Frederica paid her no heed. Her dear friend was such a headstrong young woman, but for once Dora thought she had been remarkably clever. Freddie's plan of seeking a wealthy lover had appalled Dora, but she knew how Freddie was once she got an idea into her head.

That is why the list had seemed an inspired notion, rattling off the names of all those gentlemen, but pointing out their most disagreeable features. Freddie would be bound to be discouraged from pursuing this any further.

If only she had not listed Mr. Warfield's name. But who would have guessed that Freddie would have reacted so? Dora had been certain that she had a most pointed dislike of the man.

Now Dora could only watch Freddie's actions with mounting horror, the substitution of the girl's demure muslin for a dress with a scandalously lower neckline, the dabbing of perfume between her breasts, the application of a tiny hint of rouge to Freddie's already flaming cheeks.

Despite these alarming preparations, Dora could not help but note that Freddie did not look in the least like a young woman about to go seeking a lover. No, there was a militant sparkle to her eyes, a hard set to her chin. She looked more like a duelist about to blast some poor fellow right between the eyes.

"Oh, dear. Oh, dear," Dora murmured. But short of locking Freddie in her room, she did not know what else to do. She could only wring her hands and set up a fervent prayer that when Freddie called, Mr. Max Warfield would not be at home.

Chapter 7

The morning had begun badly for Max. He had overslept, an unusual occurrence for one accustomed to waking precisely at seven-ten, no matter how late he had been abroad the night before. Rising past noon, destroying his routine, was always a guarantee that the rest of the day would proceed on disastrous lines.

And Max noted grimly that this particular day did not seem likely to prove an exception to that rule. He could not locate his favorite dressing gown, he stubbed his toe against the doorjamb leading into his dressing room, there was no fresh soap, and his French valet was nowhere to be found.

Max stripped off his nightshirt and stumbled over to the washstand. Georges had at least fetched up the bathing water, though by now it was tepid. Squinting at the flood of sunlight pouring through the latticed windows, Max scraped up what was left of the soap and proceeded to lather his arms and neck. He winced as he did so. Every muscle in his body was stiff and aching, a headache throbbing behind his temples.

He felt just like—like— His mouth quirked into a sardonic grimace. He felt just like a man who had been bashed over the head last night and knocked down in a gutter. Freddie's companion, friend, *dragon*, whatever she was, Miss Dora Applegate possessed quite a hefty right arm.

Max closed his eyes, longing for nothing more than to drag his battered frame back into bed. But it was already approaching the hour of one, and he recollected the promise he had made to Sir Pollack Sprague to ride out with him to see about the purchase of that horse. Max did not know what misplaced burst of good fellowship had induced him to make such a pledge. Sir Pollack was a most congenial fellow, but Max well knew he was not in the mood to tolerate that much cheerfulness.

And after finishing with Sir Pollack, Max was going to have to call upon his sister. That in itself was enough to dampen the prospect of any day. But he was placed in the awkward position of admitting that Caroline had been right. Something did need to be done about Freddie. Max hoped that Caroline would have enough sense not to look too smug over his capitulation, but he doubted it.

She would not gloat for long when Max informed her that he had decided Freddie was about to become her houseguest. Caroline would be less than pleased with his decision, but Max would take great pleasure in reminding her that his interference in this matter had been *her* idea.

With a low growl, Max groped for the towel to dry himself. He needed to make arrangements to have Freddie moved to Caroline's as soon as possible. A rather daunting task, he was forced to admit, because he had taken enough of Freddie's measure last night to know that she would not tamely acquiesce.

She had as good as told him to get out and not come back, to mind his own business. That was something Max was normally very good at, and he would have been happy to oblige except—

Except he could not forget how she had looked when she had squared off with him, the fragility of her features at odds with the mulish set of her chin, that spark of desperation in her blue eyes, as volatile as a fuse burning too near its end. God knows when she "went off" what mischief she might get into next time.

And what damned contradictory feelings the girl aroused in him. He had been irritated by her antics, gaming and flirting with the likes of General Sir Mordant Fortescue. And yet when he thought of her circumstances, cast off penniless by her late husband's family, living in that practically empty house with only a dithery spinster for company, forced to steal her own supper . . . his heart melted. Poor Freddie, once more his abandoned little orphan girl. He wanted to scoop her up in his arms and cradle her against him. He wanted to seize her fiercely and shake some sense into her.

Max felt a surge of anger at this Sir Wilfred Barry whom he had never met, anger at Freddie for being too damn proud to let anyone know how badly off she had been left. He was also angry at his sisters Caroline and Elizabeth, at his cousin Jameson, all of them so concerned about the family reputation, none of them having the wit to perceive Freddie's plight.

And, yes, he was angry with Max Warfield, callous bastard that he was for not inquiring after Freddie sooner, perhaps years and years sooner. Guilt was not an emotion he was comfortable with. Scowling, he raged over to his wardrobe, muttering under his breath because he still could not find his favorite dressing gown.

He was obliged to shrug into one of dark blue

wool, the fabric further irritating him by abrading his skin. He cursed again when he discovered that Georges had not yet appeared with hot water for shaving.

"Rise late one morning," he muttered savagely, "and the entire damn household decides to take a holiday."

Georges knew Max did not like to have to speak to anyone before breakfast, let alone bellow for his valet. Max strode impatiently from the dressing room back into his bedchamber, only pausing in front of the glass mounted upon the wall. He wondered if he looked as hellacious as he felt.

He did. A night's growth of beard grizzled his jaw, dark circles cast shadows under his eyes, and the knot on his temple had formed into a bruise the most alarming hue of purple. Recoiling in disgust from his own reflection, Max did not glance up when he heard the door glide open softly.

"Bloody well about time, Georges," Max growled.

His valet had enough sense not to reply. As he heard Georges creep farther into the room, Max snatched up a comb and dragged it through his disheveled black hair. He experimented, attempting to plaster the strands across his temple, covering up the bruise.

"Dreadful," a voice purred, startling Max into dropping the comb. Those sultry tones definitely did not belong to Georges. "Leave it alone. I like the bruise. It makes you look like a prizefighter."

"What the deuce!" Max whipped around, staring at the apparation leaning up against the frame of his four-poster—a golden-haired angel gowned in white, a crimson shawl draped around her shoulders. Her blue eyes glinted at him through the thickness of downswept lashes in a manner calculated to fire his blood.

He caught his breath, still unable to credit his eyes, wondering exactly how hard he had been hit over the head last night. As he stood gaping, the angel eased her shawl away, letting it drop to the floor, and Max felt an involuntary shudder rack through him.

No. Certainly no angel. No respectable cherub ever had a robe that clung like that sheer muslin over the swell of delectable curves. But he was obliged to admit, momentarily distracted by the low neck of the gown, the view was heavenly.

Then he gave himself a brisk shake, bringing his wayward masculine senses to order with a snap. "F-Freddie," he croaked. "What—what the—"

"Hullo, Max." She offered him a crooked smile, her offhand words overbright and a shade defiant.

"What the devil are you doing here!"

His explosive greeting did not appear to disconcert her. If she was at all nervous, the only sign of it was the way she played with one lock of hair, twisting it until it became a curl, lying tantalizingly along the ivory column of her neck.

"You said last night you were coming to call upon me. I thought I would save you the trouble."

"Have you lost your mind?" Max asked.

"I don't think so. How about you?" Freddie's head tilted, regarding him with unabashed curiosity.

Max suddenly recalled that he was clad in nothing but his dressing gown. It was strange. He could have paraded in the buff before the likes of a Lavinia Channing without a blush. But Freddie's innocent regard afflicted him with a rare attack of modesty.

He caught himself fumbling with the belt, drawing the folds of the robe tighter as he blustered, "You—you little idiot. Have you no notion of propriety? You cannot come calling upon an unmarried man in this fashion."

"Oh?" Freddie dimpled into a mischievous smile. "Would it be all right if you were married, then?"

Max glared at her. "How did you get past Crispin?"

"Your butler? I merely told him I was your—um—very dear cousin and that you were expecting me. I could find my own way up."

"That useless popinjay." Max swore under his breath. "He'd make a better man milliner or dancing master than he does a butler."

"I thought he was very sweet."

"Then you are a remarkably poor judge of character as well as everything else. I cannot believe you were stupid enough to come here. Calling upon a single gentleman alone would be bad enough, but—"

"I am not alone," Freddie interrupted. "Dora is with me."

"The Valkyrie? Wonderful! That is all I need. I'd best go don my armor at once."

"The armor won't be necessary, but some breeches perhaps."

Freddie had the effrontery to laugh when Max felt the red creep into his cheeks. She said, "You need not worry about Dora, in any event. Mr. Crispin is serving her tea belowstairs."

"Which is where you should be." Max strode purposefully forward, but Freddie evaded his grasp for her arm. To his complete horror, she flopped back on his unmade bed, stretching out upon the sheets with a languid sigh.

"Why are you making such a fuss, Max? We are cousins, after all. I remember once after one of our outings, you even stayed late enough to tuck me in at night. You tickled me so unmercifully that I fell off the bed and I was not the least bit sleepy. Aunt Jameson was furious."

"You are now too old for tickling games, so I would appreciate it if you would get off my bed and—" Max pulled up short, frowning. "This is the second time you have let something like that slip. Are you still going to insist you don't remember me?"

Freddie's teasing smile faded, her lashes fluttering down to conceal the expression in her eyes. "Ah, well, I suppose memories have a habit of coming back to one like—like bad dreams."

Max stared at her hard. He had a strong suspicion that nothing had come back to Freddie, that she had remembered him quite well all along. So why had she pretended otherwise? And what was all this nonsense this morning? After their parting last night, he had half expected he would have to go in search of her. Instead of indicating any desire to see him again, she had fairly told him to go to the devil.

What, then, had induced her to turn up in this startling manner? Far from darting scorn and fury, she was almost playful. She was up to some mischief, that was certain, but what it might be, he could not think.

That might be because of her perfume. As he leaned over the bed, he caught a whiff of it, the sweet odor of violets seeming to curl around his brain, threatening to steal his reason.

He gazed down at her, her golden hair tumbled against his pillow. Her breasts strained against the fabric of her dress, so damned thin, she might well be in her nightgown. Sprawled upon his bed, a faint flush colored her cheeks, her eyes as blue as a crystal clear sea. A man could get lost in their depths,

Max thought. She was both innocent and seductress, a lethal combination if ever there was one.

He felt his throat go suddenly dry, the stirrings she roused in him neither cousinly nor gentlemanly. But inevitable. Damnation. Whatever devilment she contemplated, she should have had more sense. She had been married. She ought to know what behavior such as this could do to a man. But then, Freddie did not think of him that way. He was just Cousin Max, one of her old, doddering relatives. And he needed to get her the deuce out of there before he was tempted to show her otherwise.

Reaching down, he seized her by both wrists and hauled her roughly to her feet. "All right, I have had enough of this nonsense, Freddie. Tell me what you are really doing here, and I warn you not to trifle. I am in a very dangerous mood."

"So am I." Her eyes glinted up at him, hard and bright as sapphires.

Max discovered that in dragging her off the bed, he had pulled her closer than he had intended. The soft, appealing curve of her mouth was barely inches away. He forced his gaze from the tempting outline of her moist lips, his eyes drifting lower—a mistake. He found himself looking down the front of her bodice, contemplating the satiny swell of her breasts. A shaft of fire spread through him, and he released her as though he had been scorched.

Snatching up her shawl, he attempted in clumsy fashion to arrange it back around her shoulders. She made no effort to help.

"You must be mad," he groused. "Running around dressed in a damned bed sheet."

"White muslin is all the rage," she said sweetly. "Very proper for morning wear."

It might have been if she had worn some lace to fill in the bodice, and if she had not, as Max strongly suspected, dampened her petticoats to make them cling with a shocking transparency.

He started to express further disapproval of her apparel when he was interrupted by a soft footfall outside the door, a brief tap at the wood. It was most definitely Georges this time.

Cursing, Max wheeled to the door to intercept the man.

"Good morning, m'sieur," Georges piped cheerfully. Attempting to step across the threshold, carrying a pitcher of hot water and a towel, he looked puzzled to find Max barring his path. "*Mille pardons* for my tardiness. I—"

"Never mind. I'll take that." Max grabbed both the pitcher and the towel from him. "I can shave myself this morning."

The little Frenchman actually paled at the prospect. "But, m'sieur—"

"Do you think I cannot?" Max asked fiercely.

"No, m'sieur! Er—ah, well, perhaps. Er—yes."

The valet was still babbling as Max slammed the door in his face. Max cringed at his own guilty behavior, slinking around as though something were going on in this bedchamber, as though there were something to hide. It was ridiculous in any case. Georges might not have been aware of Freddie's presence, but he soon would be. Some of the other servants, Crispin at least, would know she had come upstairs.

Max's idea had been to preserve her reputation, not to help destroy it. He turned angrily, then emitted a groan. Freddie had used the interval to discard the shawl again and her sandals as well.

She had curled up on an upholstered armchair near the fireplace, her legs tucked beneath her, her bare toes peeking out from the hem of her dress in a way that was both childlike and incredibly alluring.

"Get out of here," he roared. "Downstairs now! Until I am finished dressing."

Any of his servants would have flown to obey when he spoke in that tone. Freddie merely yawned, stretching her arms with the lazy contentment of a drowsy kitten.

"I thought I could stay and help you shave."

"I wouldn't trust you anywhere near me with a razor," he said. Stalking to the dresser, he slapped the pitcher down with such force, some of the hot liquid spattered up at him. Muttering curses, he dabbed at himself with the towel.

She straightened as though preparing to rush to him. "Oh, did you hurt yourself?"

"No! You—you just stay where you are."

She subsided back into the chair with a tiny shrug. "You seem very edgy, Max. One would think you were not accustomed to having women around."

"Women, yes. You, no!" He flung down the towel, then swiveled to face her, fists propped against his hips. "Of course, I have an idea what this is all about."

Her brows rose a fraction. "Do you indeed?"

"Yes. I annoyed you last night by pointing out some home truths, that the notion you could take care of yourself was madness and that I intended to put a stop to your recklessness. I believe this absurd visit is simply a way of getting some of your own back, of tormenting me. But you should take care, Freddie. Such amusements have a way of backfiring."

A flash of anger appeared in her eyes, a sudden rise in color in her cheeks. Max figured his accusation must have hit somewhere near the mark. But she kept her smile fixed firmly in place.

"Why, how astute you are, Max. I will admit you did . . . irritate me a trifle. But I have been thinking—"

"God save us all!"

She ignored his interjection. "You were right. I cannot continue on as I have been. But the suggestion you put forward, that I go live with your sister, did not please me. I have come up with a plan of my own."

He flung up his hands in exasperation, then drew up a wing-back chair and plunked himself down opposite her. "Well," he said impatiently. "Let's hear it. What is it?"

She did not answer immediately, but dropped her gaze as though suddenly transfixed by the pattern on the carpet. When she finally raised her eyes, she drew in a deep breath, saying almost diffidently, "I heard they are laying bets at White's as to who your next mistress will be. That Lady Channing is the odds-on favorite. Is that true?"

For a moment, Max was utterly confounded by this abrupt change of subject. He scowled. "That's none of your affair. Respectable women are not even supposed to know about such things."

Freddie rolled her eyes and sighed. "Men are so naive. And I am not in the least respectable.

"So it is true?" she persisted. "Are you looking for a mistress? Would you be willing to consider someone else besides Lady Channing?"

"I am hardly planning on taking applications for the position, but—" He broke off, annoyed. "This is a damned outrageous conversation, and I don't see what this has to do with you. I thought we were discussing your future."

"So we are. I was wondering if you might be interested in—" She paused, fretting her lower lip.

"Interested in what?"

"Interested in having me as your mistress," she blurted out.

Max was glad he was sitting down. Feeling like he had just taken an unexpected blow to the gut, he roared out, "You! My mistress! I'd sooner stare down the mouth of a loaded cannon. Where did you get such a bacon-brained notion?"

She flinched a little at his harsh words, but lifted her chin stubbornly. "It is obvious I have no talent for cards and you seem to think I need a protector."

"I didn't mean that sort of protection. Good God, when I offered to help you out of your difficulties, you cannot think that I intended . . . that you—"

"Why not?" she said softly. She shoved to her feet and glided toward him, her step a little unsteady but determined. Before he could divine her intent, she eased herself onto his knee, draping her arms around his neck.

"Don't you find me at all attractive?" she whispered.

Attractive? A bolt of lightning seemed to have shot through him at the close contact of her body against his. He could feel the warmth of her thighs pressing upon his lap, even through the layers of muslin and wool. He took a shuddering breath. If she knew anything at all about men, she would soon have no doubt about the level of his attraction to her. It was rising beneath his robe this very minute.

Squirming, he sought to pry her arms away. "Behave yourself, Freddie. Before I put you over my knee and give you a sound spanking."

"I am not a little girl anymore," she said huskily.

"No, but you are still very much a little fool."

"Is this so foolish?" she asked, snuggling closer. His efforts to thrust her away were nonavailing. But he was no longer trying very hard. Her head bent lower, her golden hair cascading over him, brushing against his cheek as she dared to steal a kiss from the taut line of his mouth. It was barely a whisper, shy and tremulous enough to break what remained of Max's self-control.

Instead of pushing her away, he crushed her hard against him, taking possession of her lips with a ruthless fervor. He caught one hand in the silky tangle of curls at the nape of her neck. Holding her captive, his mouth greedily devoured hers. Never had he felt a rush of desire, so hot, so intense, so sweet. Never had a kiss left him so profoundly shaken, hungering for more.

It was Freddie who brought him to his senses. He became aware of her hands pressed against his chest, fluttering like some delicate moth struggling to be free. He released her enough that she drew back her head with a tiny gasp. Through the mist of his own passion, he saw her eyes, wide, innocent, stunned. For all her bravado, she was nothing but a little girl playing with fire. And he had come damned close to accommodating her.

A ripple of disgust for himself tore through Max. Angry, ashamed, he thrust her away, standing up so abruptly, she tumbled to the carpet. He stepped past her, not trusting himself to touch her again.

He stalked to lean against the dresser, gulping in cleansing breaths, seeking to regain his composure, his mind reeling. What the blazes had happened to him? He had nearly allowed himself to be seduced by his cousin. By his poor, orphaned, *helpless* little cousin, he thought mockingly.

When he turned back, Freddie was getting shakily to her feet. She was pale, two spots of color branding her cheeks, but she looked a damn sight more composed than he felt at the moment. She smoothed out skirts, saying with forced cheerfulness, "Well! Does—does this mean you found me satisfactory or not?"

"Satisfactory?" Max nearly choked, giving his anger free rein. It was far safer channeling the fire that yet coursed through his veins into fury. "Damn it, Freddie! Stop talking that way, do you hear? You provoke me beyond endurance. What sort of man do you think I am that I would take advantage of my own cousin?"

She raised her head proudly. "No one takes advantage of me. If you insist upon thrusting your help on me whether I want it or not, I simply thought to make it a more fair arrangement for both of us."

"By offering yourself to me like some Haymarket doxy? I wasn't looking for that sort of repayment, Frederica."

She flinched, but shot back, "I don't accept charity anymore, Max."

"It wasn't that either, blast you. I insisted upon helping you because . . . because . . ." Max rubbed his throat, near strangling on the admission, the sort of words he ever found hardest to say. "Because I care about you, damn it."

A glitter of angry tears sparkled in Freddie's eyes. "Yes, I recall you once saying something along those lines to me. What was it now?"

"I love you, Freddie," she mimicked. *"Come in out of the rain."* She swallowed hard. "I can get myself in out of the storm these days, thank you very much, Mr. Max Named-After-Nobody-in-Particular."

Her words stunned him. He was not surprised so much that she remembered. He had already suspected that. But the depth of bitter unhappiness that obviously accompanied her memories of him disturbed him greatly.

124

Ducking her head, she tried to head for the door, but he barred her path, catching hold of her shoulders. "Freddie, I—I did mean those words when I said them."

"Yes." She sniffed, the tears coming freely. She averted her head, trying not to let him see. "Then you just went away and never came back."

He frowned. "There were . . . circumstances beyond my control."

His excuse sounded lame and far too vague. Her accusing glance told him that she thought so, too. But even after all this time, Max was astonished to find the memory of his youthful folly, his subsequent exile, raw and painful, difficult to share. As he struggled for some way to explain this to her, she waved him aside.

"Never mind, Max. The past is no longer important to me. I do not know why I bothered to mention it. And as to you refusing my offer . . ." She shrugged. "You are not the only rake in London."

Despite her tears, there was a hard, determined light in her eyes that made him uneasy. "And just what the devil is that supposed to mean?"

"Only that Dora made me up a whole list of wealthy gentlemen who might be interested in acquiring a mistress. General Fortescue, for instance."

"Fortescue!" Max hissed. "If you set one foot near that old rip again, I'll—"

He never had the opportunity to finish his threat. He and Freddie were both startled by a frantic rapping at the bedroom door.

Max swore and Freddie turned away, mopping hastily at her damp eyes. As the hammering continued without ceasing, Max strode toward the door and flung it open, preparing to tell Georges or whoever to go to the deuce.

He was nearly knocked over as Miss Dora Applegate barreled into the room. "G-good morning, Mr.
Warfield," she stammered, absurdly polite under
the circumstances. Her greeting broke off in a gasp
as she fully took in Max clad only in his robe. In
her shock, she left the bedchamber door standing
open behind her.

Wrenching her attention to Freddie, Dora cried,
"Oh, my dear. Calamity! We must get out of here.
One of Mr. Warfield's friends has come calling. Mr.
Crispin is trying to get rid of him, but he is being
quite insistent."

"Sir Pollack." Max groaned. "Come about the
horse. What damnable timing."

Dora clutched at Freddie's sleeve. "We must not
be seen here. Think of your reputation, my dear."

Freddie gave a shrug, at once listless and defiant.
"What of it?"

Dora eyed her with reproach. "You said that even
wicked women must be discreet."

"Yes, it would be better for both of you—" Max
began. But he never finished, for Sir Pollack's
cheerful voice could be heard, carrying up the
stairs. ". . . cannot believe the lazy fellow is still
abed. 'Tis most unlike Max. Don't worry, Crispin.
I am not afraid to beard the lion in his den. I'll
roust your master out myself."

Thunderation, Max thought, ready to tear out his
own hair. The fellow was already on his way up.
Thinking quickly, Max rapped out a command to
Freddie and her companion, "Both of you just stay
here. I will intercept Sir Pollack and get rid of him."

"Oh, that won't be necessary," Freddie said. "I
have met Sir Pollack before. I look forward to re-
newing my acquaintance with the gentleman."

She started toward the bedchamber door, her
hurt and anger not quite masked by her tight-lipped

smile. She looked reckless enough to do or say anything that would whistle her own reputation down the wind.

Max saw he had no time to argue with her. He did not think, did not hesitate, but overtook her in several quick strides. Before she could even cry out, he seized her around the waist. Hustling her toward the dressing room, he shoved her through the door and turned the key in the lock.

The doorknob rattled with the force of Freddie's fury and indignation. "Damn you, Max. Open this door at once, do you hear?"

"*Damn you*, Freddie. Be quiet, or I'll come in there and box your ears."

"Ohhh, yes, Freddie," Dora cried. "Do be still. Sir Pollack is almost here. We've got to hide."

Max stiffened. He had been so concerned about dealing with Freddie, he had forgotten her companion. He saw that Miss Applegate was waxing frantic to the point of hysteria. She glanced wildly around for another place of concealment, then made a dive for Max's bedstead, struggling to conceal her large frame behind the bed curtains.

"Miss Applegate!" Max said sternly. "Don't be absurd. I will unlock the door and you must go into the other room with Freddie. Miss Applegate?"

But he might as well have been talking to himself. Dora had a death grip on the curtains and would not come out. Max felt himself rapidly losing control of the situation, a sensation he hated. At least, thank God, he could be grateful for one thing. Freddie had finally shown the good sense to lapse into silence.

Max moved to haul Dora out by force and send her into the dressing room, when he froze at the sound of his friend's cheery voice.

"Max?"

Sir Pollack Sprague hesitated on the threshold, peering through the open door, a broad grin spreading over his good-humored countenance. There was nothing for Max to do but position himself in front of the bed with assumed casualness, trying not to look like a schoolboy who had been caught kissing the parlor maid.

"I trust I am not intruding?" Sir Pollack said.

"Oh, no," Max muttered. "The amount of traffic coming through here, my bedchamber might well be a turnpike. I am thinking of charging tolls."

Sprague laughed, bringing up a quizzing glass to inspect Max's attire. "Stap me, but it is true. Crack-of-dawn Warfield still in his dressing gown and 'tis near mid-afternoon."

Max rubbed his unshaven jaw, self-conscious. "You will have to excuse me. I had rather a bad night. If you would wait below, I—"

But Sir Pollack only stepped farther into the room. "I should say you did have quite a time from that knot on your head. You left the Channings early enough. It must have been one devil of party you went on to. And you didn't take me!"

Max managed a stiff smile for his friend's raillery. He was trying to act natural, but it was difficult since he had just realized the edge of Dora's petticoats and the tips of her serviceable country-style boots were showing beneath the bed curtain.

"You can be thankful you were not with me," Max said, moving to take Sir Pollack's arm and guide him firmly back into the hall. "I will tell you all about it sometime. I am sorry I forgot our appointment. I should have sent word, but I must further crave your pardon and beg off. Something has come up."

"Or down, as the case may be." Sir Pollack emitted a soft whistle. Max did not know what Sprague meant until he bent to retrieve something from the floor. Freddie's shawl, the telltale scent of her perfume lingering in its folds. Sir Pollack gave an appreciative sniff.

"Beg pardon, old man," he said jovially. "It appears I truly have interrupted something."

"Nothing at all," Max growled. "That belongs to—to my sister. She left it the last time she was here."

Unfortunately at that moment, a loud sneeze issued from the bedstead. Sir Pollack's gaze traveled to where he could no longer miss the quivering bulge behind the curtain.

He smirked. "Your sister appears to have caught a chill."

"A highly contagious one." Max tried again to steer his friend from the room, but Sir Pollack shook him off playfully. He regarded Max with a mock wounded expression.

"Max, you cannot mean to be so uncivil. Would you send me away without presenting me to your—er—sister?"

Max gave him a killing glare, but Sprague only grinned.

"After all, I wagered a handsome sum myself upon whom your next light o' love would be. I laid my blunt that you would reconcile with Mademoiselle Vivani. You have to tell me. I know I must be right. There could not be another female so tall in all of London."

"You should not bet on that. Now, come along, Sprague."

To Max's dismay, Sir Pollack skittered over to the bed, his eyes full of mischief. "Mademoiselle," he called. "Remember me? Sir Pollack Sprague. We met at a supper one evening after the opera." He reached out to tweak at the curtain. "Don't think me rude, but if I could have but one glimpse of your enchanting face to confirm . . ."

"Sprague!" Max snarled out a warning, but it was too late.

Sir Pollack had already peeked behind the curtain. Dora's pale face emerged, the feather on her drab bonnet bent down so that it tickled her nose, causing her to sneeze again.

Sir Pollack's eyes popped. He glanced toward Max with an expression of ludicrous dismay, then back to Dora, who was earnestly puffing at the feather, trying to get it off her face.

Red-faced Sir Pollack moved away, nearly stumbling over his own feet. "I—I beg your pardon, madam. Uh, Max, I thought—this is . . . I didn't—Perhaps I had—had best call again at a more opportune time."

"Perhaps you had."

"Right." Pollack nodded, half sketched Dora an awkward bow, then bolted from the room.

"Oh! Oh, dear," Dora moaned, sagging down on the edge of the bed.

"That sums up the situation quite aptly," Max said dryly.

She pressed her hands to her face. "What that man must have thought! I really am a wicked woman now." She did not look distressed so much as awestricken. "Whatever has this done to my reputation?"

"I don't know. But I can imagine quite clearly what it has done to mine." Max grimaced. He was fond of farce. But he preferred it confined to Drury Lane, not running rampant through his bedchamber.

"I am sorry, Miss Applegate." He apologized gruffly. "I will find Sir Pollack and explain."

130

"Truly. What are you going to tell him?" Dora asked with genuine interest.

Max hadn't the damnedest notion. "I will think of something. Meantime, you'd best collect Freddie. Take her home and keep her there until I straighten out this damnable coil."

Dora nodded. Still flustered from her encounter with Sir Pollack, Max was not sure she was even attending him. He moved to fetch Freddie himself, unlocking the dressing room door. Freddie was being amazingly quiet, but she still might be furious enough to fly at him like a mad cat. Cautiously, Max thrust his head into the room and called her name.

There was no response, the room silent and undisturbed, except for his wardrobe door propped open, his clothes tumbled out from his previous search for his dressing gown.

Max's eyes narrowed. He did not recall having left that great of a mess. It had to have been Freddie. Now what mischief had she been about and, more to the point, where the deuce could she have gone?

The only other way out was— Max felt a chill pass through him, his gaze focusing on the window. One of them stood open, a makeshift rope of his own white shirts knotted together, trailing over the sill.

No, impossible. This was the second story. Freddie wouldn't. She couldn't have.

Max hastened over to the window, his heart pumping as he looked out and down. He expected he scarce knew what, Freddie clinging perilously to the side of the house or worse yet, her slender frame broken on the garden walk below. But nothing stirred beneath him except for Thornton, the gardener, hunched over to weed the flower beds.

Max started to call out to him, but thought better of it. The old man was half deaf. Besides, when Thornton was absorbed with his precious roses, the sky could be raining golden-haired young women and the gardener would not notice a thing.

Freddie had obviously made good her escape. Drawing up the precarious rope which had aided her flight, Max could only be grateful he had spared no expense upon his shirts, that the linen had been sturdy enough to withstand bearing Freddie's weight.

The little idiot, Max thought savagely. She could have snapped her neck. However had she contrived to knot the shirts so tightly together? As if that were of any importance.

All that mattered was that Freddie was gone, leaving so much between them unsettled. Feeling frustrated and strangely bereft, Max yanked the window closed, silently cursing the day he had ever taught that girl to climb.

Chapter 8

Whatever dignity was left to Freddie after her encounter with Max she was obliged to part with upon the following day. It was hard to be dignified struggling with someone over the possession of a ham.

Bracing herself upon the threshold of her kitchen door, Freddie barred entrance to the butcher's apprentice, who balanced the large slab of meat in his muscular arms.

"I told you," Freddie snapped for the third time. "You have the wrong house."

The burly youth only grinned at her, handsome in his way despite the shaggy lengths of brown hair tumbling across his eyes. His gaze was bold, the apron knotted around Freddie's waist obviously deceiving him as to her position in the household.

"And I told you, sweeting," he said. "Been born and raised in London. Bill Tolliver never mistakes an address. Now, why don't you scoot your pretty self upstairs and ask your mistress? I'll wager she knows how this order came about."

"I am the mistress of this house," Freddie said icily. "And I assure you I know nothing whatsoever of any ham, nor can I—er—nor do I intend to pay for it."

The lad assumed a somewhat more respectful stance. "Beg pardon ma'am. But this here ham is a gift, courtesy of one o' your gentleman admirers."

"A gift? From whom?" Freddie demanded, although she had a sinking feeling she already knew the answer.

"A Mr. Maxmillian Warfield." The young man retained enough impudence to wink at her. "A most practical sort of gent. A good slab of bacon's better than posies, eh?"

Freddie felt her cheeks flame. She bit back the urge to inform the youth that Max Warfield was no "gent," and as for the rest, she very much doubted Max had any admiration left for her after yesterday's scene in the bedchamber.

She wanted to step back and slam the door in the lad's smirking face, but that was a little difficult considering that the rest of her household had already gathered in the kitchen. Dora, Till, balancing the baby on her hip, even the squinting Stubbins, all regarded the ham with varying degrees of wistfulness.

The matter, however, was decided when Master Jack whooped into the kitchen, exclaiming, "Ham! Stap me, of all things my favorite!"

Freddie thought she had no pride left, but she felt a large lump of it gather in her throat. Nonetheless, she swallowed and stepped aside, grudgingly allowing Bill Tolliver to enter.

The butcher's apprentice was hard followed by a poulter bearing a large dressed goose and, after him, the greengrocer. All courtesy of Mr. Maxmillian Warfield. Freddie found herself thrust aside in the hubbub of excitement these deliveries occasioned.

While Tolliver flirted with Till and admired the baby, Jack helped to cart in the crates of fresh fruits and vegetables with a deal of boyish enthusiasm, already crunching down upon an apple.

It astonished Freddie how quickly the boy had fit himself into their rather topsy-turvy household, cheerfully turning his hand to tasks that most noblemen's sons would have considered far beneath them. But Jack possessed a zest for any activity, a lively curiosity that led him to try anything from helping Stubbins sweep the front stoop to aiding Till in the kitchen, rattling the copper pans until they were all nigh driven to distraction.

Despite her chagrin at being forced to accept Max's latest act of charity, Freddie managed to spare the boy a brief smile before slipping quietly out of the kitchen.

Only when she passed into the dining parlor did she permit her frown to return. Absently, she stripped off the apron, soiled from her morning's efforts, trying to help Till bake two loaves of bread out of only one cup of flour.

Thanks to Max, they would not now have to worry about such shortages. But Freddie did not want to be offering any thanks to Max. Not now, not ever.

A restless night of reflection and fretting had done nothing to soften yesterday's humiliation for her. She felt her face might burn forever at the mere thought of how she had thrown herself at Max's head and been summarily rejected.

She still smarted as she recollected his blunt outburst. He would rather face a loaded cannon than have her as his mistress. But truthfully, what had she expected him to say? Had she really thought for one moment he would ever take her up on her outrageous offer?

Looking back, she did not know what madness had possessed her to approach him with such a suggestion. Perhaps Max had been right when he had questioned her motives, hinted that she had been acting partly out of a need for revenge. Never one to shrink from examining the dark corners of her own soul, Freddie was forced to admit there might be some truth in Max's words. In some perverse way, she had been trying to shock him, hurt him as he had hurt her so long ago.

Aye, that truly was the worst of it, far worse than making herself ridiculous attempting to play the role of seductress. She had let down her defenses, revealed to Max just how well she remembered him, how important those memories were, how much they still had the ability to wound her. She had let him see beyond the brittle gaiety of her careless smiles, shown him just how vulnerable she could be.

She had actually cried. Freddie winced. Good Lord, how long had it been since she had done that, wept in front of anyone? No wonder Max still viewed her as a child, and an idiotic one at that.

After that mortifying contretemps in his bedchamber, it would be gratifying never to have to see the man again. Even after her successful escape from his house, Freddie had been a bundle of nerves yesterday evening, fearful that Max would turn up, demanding to see her.

When he hadn't come then or this morning, she had told herself that she must have succeeded in disgusting him enough to leave her alone. But the ham certainly put paid to that notion, Freddie thought glumly. She obviously was not quit of Mr. Max Warfield yet. Sighing, she rubbed her temples, feeling the nigglings of another headache coming on.

The London air did not seem to agree with her. Perhaps Lady Caroline Bentley had been correct. Maybe Freddie should retire to Bath with the other elderly widows and invalids.

Realizing that she had lingered too long in the dining parlor, Freddie moved briskly forward. She hoped to steal away unnoticed, have more time to brood alone in privacy. But Freddie had waited too long to make good her escape. The parlor door swung open and Dora came bustling over to her.

"Well! If that wasn't the most provident thing in the world, the arrival of all that food," Dora exclaimed. "Like manna from heaven. I was certain we were going to have to resort to the turban again. Wasn't it simply too thoughtful of Mr. Warfield?"

"Quite," Freddie said with a grimace.

Dora's brow knit in a puzzled frown. "Though I do not quite understand it. I thought you said that Mr. Warfield had most definitely turned down your—ah—suggestion?"

"He did. This morning's bounty is charity, Dora, pure and simple." Freddie gritted her teeth. "And I shall pay him back if it takes me until the end of my days."

"Oh, dear, oh, dear! And I was hoping Mr. Warfield might call. For all his gruffness, he truly is a nice young man. But if you intend to quarrel with him again—"

"Don't fret, Dora. Perhaps Mr. Warfield will content himself with playing King Cophetua from a distance. Gentlemen do not care for scenes either, and I certainly enacted him a memorable one yesterday."

The bitterness in Freddie's voice only seemed to add to Dora's distress. Her lower lip trembled. "You must not blame yourself, Freddie. It was my fault. As your older and wiser companion, I never should have let you go to Mr. Warfield in the first place. I am so very sorry."

The notion of Dora's wisdom would have at any other time provoked Freddie with a desire to smile, but she was too overcome with shame, a sense of her own guilt.

She caught hold of Dora's hand, saying, "Don't you dare take on so, Dora. We both know full well it is I who should be apologizing to you."

"But you already did—"

"But not enough. I shall never be able to tell you I am sorry half enough. When I think of how I ran off and left you there— I always knew I was many things, but I never thought a coward was one of them."

"You aren't! You are the most courageous, brave, and loyal friend anyone could have."

Freddie only shook her head darkly, recalling how she had fled from Max's town house. At the time, she had considered herself as acting out of defiance, determined to show Max she would not tolerate being locked in like a naughty child. But in truth, she had had but one selfish thought in her head, that she could not bear to face Max again at that moment. She had not even considered what Dora might be left to deal with. Later, when Dora had described her encounter with Sir Pollack Sprague, Freddie had been and still was horrified.

She stroked a stray curl back from her older friend's brow, murmuring, "Oh, my Dora, whatever have I done to you? You led such a quiet, peaceful life at Dunhaven, and I have brought you nothing but chaos and worry, perhaps even cost you your reputation. I should not blame you if you had come to quite detest me."

"Never!" Dora cried, the ever-ready sentimental tears starting to her eyes. "What you have done for me is wonderful. Don't you see? Back at Dunhaven, I was nobody, just poor, dull, respectable Cousin Dora. I never turned any man's head, not unless one tripped over my feet."

The woman smiled mistily. "But yesterday I was actually mistaken for a wicked woman. Oh, I know it won't last. Mr. Warfield will find Sir Pollack and explain everything. He said that if Sir Pollack dared to impugn my honor, Max—that is, Mr. Warfield, would call him out even if he was his friend.

"But of course Sir Pollack will believe Max, because after all, I am not the sort of woman a gentleman would—well, but at least I shall always have the memory."

She drew herself up proudly. "For at least one afternoon in my life I was the center of a most delicious, scandalous adventure."

Freddie stared at her somberly. Until that moment, she felt she had never fully understood how bleak, how barren Dora's life must have been.

"Someday, Dora," she vowed, "I'll give you a truly grand adventure, one that will last longer than an afternoon. I'll give you—"

But she broke off, as ever haunted by the realization of their circumstances. Deflated, she concluded, "What I will most likely give you is debtor's prison and disgrace."

"Oh, no, Freddie. I am sure Mr. Warfield will not let that happen. Even though he was not so obliging as to accept your offer, he must still mean to—"

"Mr. Warfield is not the solution to our problems, Dora."

"Then what is, my dear Freddie?"

Freddie already knew the answer, and although the thought left her feeling bleak, she managed a smile and a careless hunch of one shoulder. "Oh, I suppose I must now simply make another choice from our list of rakes."

Dora's eyes widened immediately in alarm. "Oh, Freddie, now what are you planning to do?"

"I fear I have already done it," Freddie said with a sad smile. "General Fortescue sent an invitation this morning and I have accepted it. I am riding out with him this very afternoon."

Three o'clock was not the fashionable hour to go riding through St. James. The paths of the sprawling park were by and large devoid of company and it was the perfect time to arrange a clandestine meeting or a lover's rendezvous.

Freddie thought she might have had great success in making her intentions obvious to an experienced rake like General Sir Mordant Fortescue. But any flirtation was impossible, not with her companion wedged on one side of her in the open carriage, her grandson on the other.

Freddie still was not sure how it had come about that Dora and Jack had been included in the outing. If she had not known Dora to be completely without guile, she might have strongly suspected her of manuevering it thus.

As it was, Freddie supposed it had to be put down to General Fortescue's gallantry. For all his foolish little vanities and blustering manner, there was an underlying core of kindness about the man. He appeared genuinely fond of children and liked the company of women, taking a roguish delight in quizzing even the stolid Dora, putting her to the blush.

As the carriage rattled along the park's shady lanes, the general entertained them with tales of his army days, campaigns he had fought in, battles won and lost.

Freddie placed one gloved hand to her lips, trying not to yawn. Dora and Jack, however, were enthralled, Dora's admiring murmurs in particular causing the old man to puff out his chest like a pouter pigeon and continue to drone on.

Freddie supposed she should feel annoyed to find her plans so disrupted. There would be no casting out lures to the general this afternoon. Instead, she felt a half-guilty relief, like a prisoner receiving a temporary stay of execution but knowing the hanging must come eventually.

Yet today she could relax a little, even enjoy the breeze tickling her curls, soft and warm as a lover's caress. It was a perfect spring day, as though, weary of the drabness of winter, nature had become like an artist run wild, splashing the grass vivid green, streaking the sky breathtaking blue, running a rainbow riot through the flower beds.

General Fortescue commanded his driver to pull up so that they could all alight and walk along the edge of the lake. Jack insisted upon handing his "grandmama" down himself with a quaint courtliness that amused the general.

The next instant the lad charged toward the lake with a cry of heartfelt boyish delight, his arms flung wide, as though he would embrace the entire scene. He skipped along the edge, his antics causing no end of consternation among the ducks who waddled there.

The general was nearly as bad, showing the boy how to skim stones across the lake's rippling surface, make raucous noises that would set the prim swans aflutter. Dora followed after them, clucking her tongue.

"Take care, Master Jack, you will fall in. Mind where you step, General Fortescue. You will get the toes of your Hessians wet."

Her gentle scoldings filled Fortescue with a chortling delight. He laughed and slapped his thigh, saying, "We'd best heed the lady before she tweaks our ears, eh, lad? Such a solidly sensible sort of a gel." With the rest of her party so obviously entertained, Freddie was content to lag behind, absorbed by her own thoughts. She intended to proceed more subtly with the general than she had with Max. Fortescue had certainly offered her far more encouragement, enough signs of his admiration. Her experience with Leon had taught her how to get on with gentlemen of a more mature persuasion. She and the general should deal quite comfortably together.

True, the thought of their relationship assuming a more intimate nature roused no enthusiasm in her, indeed left her feeling a little cold. But surely that was better than being unnerved as she had been by Max—

Freddie felt her cheeks warm and wished she had remembered to bring her parasol. The small poke front of her bonnet was not enough to keep the sun off her face. Yet, as she moved into the shade of a towering elm, she was obliged to admit, it was not the sun heating her countenance, but a memory.

The memory of Max's kiss. Leaning up against the tree, she had only to close her eyes and she could still recall the taste, the rough, warm texture of his lips, the ruthless passion of his embrace which should have terrified her but hadn't. It had only succeeded in arousing something hot and equally hungry in herself.

And it had been *that* that had frightened her, the waking of some part of her that had been slumbering inside of her all these years, the stirrings of a hidden sensuality she had heretofore never suspected.

Leon had often laughed and warned her it would be thus one day. When he had embraced her, Freddie had once shyly admitted she found kissing sweet and very pleasant. Strangely enough, her compliment caused a momentary flash of hurt to cross his age-lined features.

"If I were twenty years younger," he had growled, his eyes lightning with a wry self-mockery. "Ah, but someday, little girl. Someday we shall see if you find kissing 'very pleasant.' " His words had been laced with sadness, resignation, and something of a tender amusement.

Freddie had never understood exactly what Leon had meant. Now she wondered if he had known that someday there would be man like Max who would teach her.

No! Freddie tensed, digging her gloved fingers against the tree bark. She had learned all from Max that she cared to, and he certainly was interested in offering no more lessons. It still seemed disloyal to Leon to be thinking such things, and yet every instinct she possessed told her that Leon would have liked Max, approved of him.

And would Leon approve of her present plans for the future regarding General Fortescue? She doubted her late husband would have been pleased by the necessity of them. But unlike Max, Leon would have understood.

Freddie sighed, a shout from Jack disrupting her reveries. Shading her eyes with one hand, she squinted along the length of the lakeshore, half expecting to find the boy had tumbled in at last. Scarce noticing her absence, her party had moved a considerable distance ahead.

Jack wasn't in the lake, but only the general's grip on the boy's coattails appeared to be restraining him. What occasioned Jack's excitement was a vehicle moving at a smart pace through the park.

Jack pointed back in the direction of the road, calling loudly enough for the whole park to hear. "Damme! What a sweet pair of goers!"

The boy was correct. Even Freddie knew a pair of perfectly matched bays when she saw them. They were hitched in the traces of a high-perched phaeton, and for a moment Freddie forgot her more troubling thoughts, lost in admiration for the way the driver handled such a spirited team.

That is, until the carriage drew close enough for her to glimpse the face of the man at the reins.

Max.

Cursing the perversity of fate, Freddie shrank back farther behind the tree. But she realized it was to no avail. Fate was not to be blamed for this particular mischance. Max appeared to be scanning the depths of the park as much as keeping an eye on the roadway. Freddie knew instinctively he was looking for her.

She also knew the instant he spotted her. Max drew back abruptly on the reins, bringing his team to a halt. Turning over the ribbons to his groom, Max had vaulted to the ground in a trice and was striding across the grass, heading purposefully in Freddie's direction.

She knew a strong impulse to run, cover the distance along the lake to catch up with the others, obliging Max to greet her in the safety of company. But if she kept giving way to these craven impulses where Max was concerned, she would end by despising herself.

She forced herself to wait, boldly watching his approach. Leon had been wont to mock the uninspiring apparel of the modern young man, preferring the flamboyant silks and brocades of his own era. But the present styles became Max well, the close-fitting dark jacket seeming designed to call attention to the power of his shoulders, the breadth of his chest. The skin-tight buckskin breeches outlined his legs so well, Freddie could tell Max had no need to resort to padding to fill out the muscular shape of his thighs.

Ashamed to be ogling him, Freddie lowered her gaze but fixed her impudent smile in place like a shield of armor. The best defense was ever a good attack, so as soon as he was within hearing range, she called out with forced merriment.

"As I live and breathe, Max Warfield. What an unlucky chance—I mean, what a coincidence. What brings you abroad at such an unfashionable hour."

But one look at the grim set of Max's mouth told her he was having none of it. He drew up alongside of her, saying, "Your butler told me where you had gone."

"I've always told Stubbins he can be forthcoming with my *friends*. But the poor man is nearsighted. I daresay he did not recognize it was *you*."

Max flinched at this jab, and Freddie was half ashamed of making it.

"We did not part on the best of terms yesterday," he said, "but you should not have run away like that."

"I suppose you were not amused by the use I made of your shirts. I trust your laundress was able to—"

"This is not about my shirts, Frederica. There were other things I badly needed to say to you."

"Truly? I suppose that is why you half beat my door down last night."

It was Max's turn to look a little ashamed. He colored slightly beneath his layering of tan. "I wanted to come last evening, but I thought better of it. It seemed wise to allow—to allow emotions some time to settle."

She angled a mocking glance from beneath the brim of her bonnet. "What, were you afraid I might make another attempt to ravish you? I suppose you need have no fear meeting me here in the park. Your cries for help would surely be answered by someone."

"It was not *your* lack of self-control that worried me." He whipped off his high-crowned beaver, jamming his fingers through his hair in a gesture rife with frustration. "Damn. I might have known you were not going to make this easy."

"A gentleman of intuition. How rare," Freddie drawled. Then she sighed. "I don't think there is anything more we have to talk about, Max. We both made our feelings plain yesterday afternoon. Now, if you will excuse me. I am not here alone. My companions will soon tire of disturbing the swans and be looking for me."

At her words, Max also turned and regarded the trio at the far bend of the lake. He peered more intently at the distant figures.

"That's Fortescue with Miss Applegate."

"I believe it is," Freddie said pleasantly.

Max eyed her with hard suspicion. "What the deuce are you doing here with him?"

Freddie smiled sweetly. "I told you about Dora's list of eligible rakes, did I not? Well, his name came after yours."

She gasped aloud as the next instant Max seized her upper arms in a bruising grip and pressed her back against the elm.

"Are you mad?" he grated. "You cannot truly be thinking of offering yourself to that old roué."

"My plans are none of your business." She raised her chin in defiance, but somehow found herself unable to meet his piercing gaze. She murmured, "You are hurting me, Max. Let me go."

He eased the pressure of his fingers, but still did not release her. "Freddie, believe me, I understand the desperation that is driving you, but there is another way. I have been talking to both of my sisters about the way you have been neglected by the family, convincing them that something must be done."

"Just doing your duty, Max?" Freddie sneered.

He ignored her interpolation. "I have told them—that is, we have all agreed you should be brought out properly in society, given another chance. You are a young and beautiful woman. Even without a great dowry you could surely achieve a respectable marriage."

Freddie squirmed, managing to wrench out of his grasp. "I don't want to be married!"

"Forgive me, but from what you hinted about your late husband, I thought you did not find marriage a disagreeable experience."

"No, it . . . it was wonderful."

"Then why not marry again?"

"Because I cheat at solitaire, not hearts!"

Her passionate response clearly puzzled him. She tried to explain. "I find what you are proposing quite cold-blooded, the idea of marrying a man for security and not affection."

Max's dark brows arched with incredulity. "And yet you talk of finding a lover by going down a list of names. If that is not cold-blooded, I scarce know what is."

"That is different," Freddie said stubbornly. "No one expects undying devotion in a mistress. It is more of a business arrangement."

"Most people would say the same of marriage."

"Well, I am not one of them. Marriage is for a lifetime, based on vows of love and fidelity. I may be flippant about many things, Max, but *I* take *my* promises very seriously."

He looked away, saying gruffly, "That is another reason I needed to speak to you. You mentioned something yesterday about broken promises, the way I once left you without ever saying good-bye."

"I was being silly." Freddie waved him off with a dismissive gesture. "There is no point in raking over old coals. It was not important."

"Obviously I hurt you very badly and you are entitled to an explanation."

"Your explanation comes years too late. I am not interested." Freddie tried for an air of icy dignity, but her voice came out sounding petulant, even childish. What was it about Max that could reduce her to the state of a hurt little girl again?

"Besides," she added, "I already know why you went away. Aunt Jameson told me."

"She did?"

"She said you had gone off to make your fortune in Jamaica."

Max essayed a hard laugh. "That was half true. But unfortunately there was a little more to it than that. I did not go. I was banished by my father, asked never to return during his lifetime."

"Good God!" Freddie exclaimed in involuntary horror. "You could not have done anything that dreadful . . . could you?"

He didn't answer, merely stared into the distance, absently shredding one of the elm leaves. Even after all these years Max was obviously very reluctant to talk about what he had done to so alienate his father.

Wild thoughts of theft, sedition, even murder chased through Freddie's brain. She half dreaded to ask, "What terrible crime did you commit?"

"I fell in love." Max turned to offer her a wry

half smile. "Your memory of that summer is obviously incomplete, Frederica. Seen through a child's eyes, you recall only pony rides and tickling games. You don't remember me wandering about like a moon-calf, sighing over the flowers, telling you ridiculous things like when I was married, I would take you to live with me."

"Yes, I—I do remember some such faradiddle."

"Aye, faradiddle is the word, and what's more I believed it myself. I truly thought by some miracle I would acquire enough of a fortune to build a mansion for me and my bride. And you. You were to come and be our little sister."

Freddie crinkled her nose. Once she would have been entranced by the thought of being Max's little sister. Now the notion struck her as extremely displeasing. At the outset she had assured herself she would be interested in nothing Max could have to say. But now she could not refrain from asking him, "And who was to be the bride, this lady who had so bewitched you?"

"She was the daughter of longtime friends of my father. A lovely, gentle girl. An heiress in her own right."

"She sounds perfect. So what was the difficulty?"

"Jane was already betrothed, her match arranged to a man of title and property. But that did not deter me. I fear I was infatuated beyond reason."

Max spread his hands in a helpless gesture, as though groping for the words to explain. "Jane admired me. And she seemed delicate and vulnerable. She made me feel so wise, the great, strong male. That's heady stuff when you're a gawky lad of eighteen, brought up to think of yourself as a person of no importance. I was special to her, not just an insignificant younger son."

You were special to me, too, Max, Freddie wanted to cry out. But pride kept her silent. She was dismayed to feel the jealousy curling inside her over a female she had never met, a lady long gone from Max's life. Gone perhaps, but from the shadows that touched his eyes, clearly not forgotten.

Sighing, Max continued. "As the time drew near for her wedding, she promised me to cry off. But with each passing day, she found some excuse, and I realized she would never have the courage to stand against the wishes of her family. In desperation I took matters into my own hands. I—I abducted her."

When Freddie stared at him, Max drew himself up defensively. "I was so certain Jane loved me. I thought once her initial fear and apprehension passed, she would see that eloping was the only way, perhaps even find some romance in the notion."

His lips drew back into a derisive smile, sneering at his own folly. "As it turned out, my love was not that romantic, nor was she that much in love with me. As I watched her lash herself into hysterics, I realized what I had mistook for gentleness was naught but weakness. Oh, she was very fond of me, enjoyed my attentions, but not enough to sacrifice her future for me. Did I not understand? Jane was not made for a life of poverty and scandal. She had been brought up to be a marchioness. That was what she wanted and I ruined everything."

Even after so many years that ages-old disillusionment seemed to weigh down upon Max, the heavy, carved lines around his mouth becoming more prominent as he concluded, "By the time her father caught up to us, I was ready to hand her back and gladly. Of course, my father came as well, so furious, I thought he would have a fit of apoplexy. He said I had disgraced my family for the last time, that he would make arrangements at once to send me to my uncle in Jamaica. At that moment he could have sent me to the devil and I would not have cared."

Freddie did not want to feel sympathy for Max, but she trembled with indignation for him all the same. "It seems a little excessive to have sent you so far away forever. I suppose it was dishonorable, trying to steal another man's bride. But you were very young, hotheaded. Surely after your lady went back and wed her lord, you could simply have stayed away from her and—"

"Ah, but you do not fully comprehend the extent of my villainy. My lady love did indeed return to her lord, who has since succeeded to his title. She is now the Marchioness of Huntley."

When Freddie furrowed her brow, still uncomprehending, he added softly, "My brother's wife."

"You had to endure losing the woman you loved to your own brother! Oh, Max." Unable to stay the impulsive gesture, she reached out, resting her hand on his wrist. "Why did you not tell me all this years ago?"

"You were only a child. You thought me some sort of blasted hero. How could I tell you such a sordid tale?"

"It was not sordid so much as very sad. And you were exiled to Jamaica all this time?"

He turned her hand over, capturing her fingers, kneading them lightly as though grateful for the contact. "More or less. Don't look so pitying. It was not that bad. I finally discovered something I was good at. I have a real head for business concerns, eventually made my fortune in shipping. I returned to England only two years ago, when my father died. I had been pretty much ignored by the entire family until then. But when I came back, well juiced, they all magnanimously forgave my past transgressions, including the fact that I had made my money in trade."

"Then I suppose you saw your brother's wife again?"

"Inevitably."

"I daresay she had grown plump, quite matronly," Freddie suggested hopefully.

"No, the years have changed Jane very little. She is as lovely as ever."

"Oh." Freddie was unable to account for the sinking feeling in the pit of her stomach.

Max continued cheerfully. "Jane is still the same flighty little ninnyhammer she always was. I expect I am the one who changed. I know you perceive me as doddering, but I assure you that the advancing years have rendered my mental perceptions only more acute."

A laugh escaped Freddie. For a moment she felt light-headed with relief. She sobered immediately, trying to ignore the fact that Max had now taken possession of both her hands.

"You could have written to me, Max. At least once in all those years. I was a very precocious child, you know. I learned to read when I was only five."

"Precocious and impertinent." He started a smile, but it faded before it ever reached his eyes. "I didn't expect that I was ever coming back to England, Freddie. I thought you would soon forget me and just as well. I was no proper companion for a little girl. I did not believe my going away could have mattered so much to you."

"It did. For a long time I did not believe Aunt Jameson when she said you would visit me no more. I watched out the nursery window, waiting every day, expecting to see you come riding down the drive." To her dismay, she felt a lump rise into her throat. She finished in a whisper, "I felt as though I had lost my only friend. It—it was as bad as when Mama and Papa had died."

Max reached out to brush the moisture from her cheek, a tear that Freddie was scarce aware had escaped.

"Forgive me," he murmured. He turned her palm upright and bent to brush a kiss upon the area of her wrist exposed by the edge of her glove. A tingling warmth shot through her, and her heart did a crazed flip-flop.

"Forgive me," he repeated, "for I will never be able to forgive myself."

Once Freddie had thought she would have given much to see Max stricken with guilt, but now her only desire was to drive the shades of remorse from his eyes.

"It was not so great a matter," she said gruffly, attempting to disguise her breathlessness, her desire to run her fingers through his crisp ebony hair as he once more caressed her throbbing pulse with his lips. "You scarcely left me a homeless waif. My uncle's estate was one of the most prominent ones in Dorchester."

"I should have made inquiries," he insisted. "Found some way to make provision for you."

"The Jamesons were very generous. I had all the advantages their daughters did, the same dolls, gowns, tutors." Freddie could not help biting down upon her lip, observing ruefully. "However, it would have been a deal more pleasant if Aunt Jameson had not always been reminding me how grateful I should be, pointing out the new pianoforte or sofa that they could have gotten if so much did not have to be spent on my support."

Max muttered something about her aunt under his breath. But Freddie was certain she could not have heard him right. No, he could not have called Aunt Jameson anything like *that*.

She shrugged. "Oh, I expect that I was the ungrateful, wicked wretch that Aunt Jameson always said. I even upset the marriage plans she had taken pains to arrange for me."

"I thought you had been quite dutiful about accepting Raincliffe."

When Freddie realized his misconception, she laughed. "Aunt Jameson never arranged my match to Leon. She thought him the most utter reprobate despite his title and money. He absolutely horrified her and took great pleasure in doing so. No, the Jamesons attempted to pair me off to a man of the utmost respectability, a sallow-faced squire with the meanest, squinty little eyes. Leon rescued me.

"I had known Leon for a long time. One of his lesser estates bordered the Jamesons'. He kept a hunting box there. I was always trespassing, stealing the apples off his trees, setting my pup into his coveys, stirring up his birds.

"I hid in his orchard the day I realized I would have to marry that dreadful squire or run away. Leon found me sitting in one of his apple trees, crying. He lifted me down and swore that he would never know another decent day's shooting again if he didn't marry me himself and teach me to be a lady."

Freddie grew misty-eyed at the memory. She became aware that Max had released her hands. His gaze was fixed on her, his expression unreadable as he said hoarsely, "You must have loved him a great deal."

"I was very fond of him. How could I have been

otherwise? He pampered me, made much of me, treated me like a princess."

"In fact, behaved just like a doting grandfather," Max said eagerly.

Freddie chuckled. "There was never anything the least grandfatherly about Leon. He used to tell me stories about his youth that would make your hair stand on end."

Max's brows knit into a heavy scowl. "Doubtless that is where you acquired all your information about mistresses and discreet arrangements."

"I certainly did not learn it from Aunt Jameson."

"It seems to me that your late husband imparted a great many notions that were improper for an innocent young bride."

"Leon was always a gentleman, but certainly not ruled by conventional behavior. In many ways he was like you, but of course, not nearly so stuffy."

"Stuffy!"

Freddie thought Max would choke on the word, and her lips parted in a self-satisfied smile. "Aye, for a rakehell, Max, I find you incredibly prudish."

"Only where you are concerned."

"I think I liked you better in the days of your wild youth," Freddie mused teasingly. "You taught me so many useful things."

Max quirked one brow. "Such as how to climb out second-story windows?"

She had the grace to blush. "I suppose I ought to apologize for my—er—precipitous departure yesterday. But I don't take kindly to being locked in."

"I only wanted to keep you—" He broke off ruefully. "I seem to make so many mistakes where you are concerned. And you have never yet said whether you will forgive me or no."

Freddie stared deep into the mists of his gray

eyes. If he persisted in regarding one in that bone-melting way, a woman would be apt to forgive him anything. No wonder he was styled as the most eligible rake in London.

She held out her hand to him in what she hoped was casual fashion. "Gracious, I am not the sort to hold a grudge, Max. From herein, I do hope we can be friends again."

He shook hands with her, retaining possession longer than was necessary. His eyes lit with amusement. "I should warn you about that. I no longer give my friendship lightly. But when I do, I am told that I can be high-handed and damnably interfering."

"You already are."

Max had no opportunity to reply to this riposte, for they both became aware that they no longer stood alone beneath the elm's spreading leaves.

Jack came tearing up, his round face red and perspiring with excitement. "Faith, lady, look what I have found." He held up one hand, an ugly specimen of a caterpillar inching along his stubby finger.

"Ugh. How perfectly charming." Freddie grimaced.

Max looked a little irritated at being interrupted. He flicked a glance over the boy. "And who might this young rogue be?"

Jack returned Max's frown, his own deepening to a scowl when his gaze slid pointedly to where Max still retained Freddie's hand.

"More to the point, who are you, sir?" Jack said, forgetting the caterpillar as he drew himself up. "I believe I must request you to unhand my grandmama."

"Your grandmama?" Max relaxed to a stance of

wary amusement. When Jack glowered, Freddie stepped quickly into the breach with introductions.

"Jack, this is Mr. Warfield, the owner of that bang-up rig you so recently admired. Max, this is my grandson, St. John Bartholmew Barry, otherwise known as Jack."

"Mr. Barry to you, sir," Jack said with a stiff bow.

Max's lazy grin had slowly faded as he whipped to face Freddie. "What! You don't mean Sir Wilfred's son."

"Yes, his youngest, in fact."

"Frederica! I heard rumors in my club only this morning. A search has been set up for that boy since he turned up missing from school."

"I am not missing," Jack growled. "I am with my grandmama."

Freddie laughed, but Max did not look in the least diverted. Dark lights of annoyance sparked into his eyes, his lips setting in a determined clamp, all signs which Freddie had come to recognize as heralding trouble.

"By God, Frederica," he said. "When I locked you in yesterday, I should have thrown away the key and boarded up the windows. You are insane. Abducting Sir Wilfred's son."

"I didn't," she cried. "He came to me."

"Then you should have had the sense to—never mind," he ground out. " 'Tis clearly one more coil for me to untangle."

Something in the tone of Max's voice caused Freddie to encircle her arm protectively about Jack's shoulders.

"And just what do you think you are going to do?" she challenged.

"First, I am seizing Master Jack here by the collar and marching him back to school." Max leveled a grim look in her direction. "And then, by God, madam, I shall return to deal with you."

Chapter 9

Max realized he was not the most popular fellow at the moment. As he paced the confines of Freddie's parlor, he scanned the faces of his companions. Friendlier countenances were more likely to be found on the faces of a mob crowding around the base of a guillotine.

Dora perched on the chaise lounge, sniffing into a handkerchief, pausing only long enough to glare balefully at Max. The hand that Freddie had so recently extended in friendship was now clenched into a tight fist. Even General Fortescue looked as though Max had just kicked his favorite dog.

Frowning, Max drummed his fingers on the mantelpiece, waiting for the boy to make his reappearance. Master Jack had been dispatched abovestairs to make himself ready for the journey. Max had had some qualms about trusting the feisty youth out of his sight, but the boy had swept him a scorn-filled glance, saying, "You have my word that I will not attempt to run off, sir. And *I* am a gentleman."

There was something touching about the way the child squared his shoulders, managing a certain dignity despite the snub nose and dusting of freck-les. But Max steeled himself against any softer feelings, refusing to give way to the spell that young Jack appeared to have cast over the rest of the household.

The silence in the drawing room stretched out to the point of being unbearable until it was at last broken by Dora, who cried, "Oh, Mr. Warfield, I simply do not understand how you can be so cruel."

"Cruel, madam?" Max shot her a look rife with impatience. "Call it, rather, common sense, and you should be thankful that I, at least, have some. You are lucky that Sir Wilfred has not swooped down upon all of you, bringing the authorities with him. There are laws against keeping a boy hidden from his father. The only reason you have not been discovered is that Sir Wilfred has been so cautious, keeping his inquiries after the boy most discreet."

The general pulled a face of disgust. "Aye, that in itself shows what sort of father he is. B'gad, if it had been m'lad who had gone missing, I would have upended all of England searching for him."

Privately, Max agreed with him, although he said aloud, "I daresay Sir Wilfred hopes to avoid stirring up any gossip."

"I daresay he does," Freddie said tartly. "Wilfred would hardly want the world to know that he neglected his own son so badly, the child felt obliged to run away. That would be quite a nuisance, so troublesome to poor Wilfred."

Max frowned at her. "Trouble that, as usual, appears ready to land on your doorstep."

"I have a penchant for it, which you obviously do not. I will say to you the same thing I did when we left the park, Max. Stay clear of this. Let me handle the problem with Jack."

"You have yet to make any effort to do so and you have had the boy with you for two whole days."

Freddie flushed. "I—I will write to Sir Wilfred this very day. I promise."

"No, Frederica. I think not. The boy goes with me."

Freddie eyed him with complete frustration, but it was the general who thrust himself forward, blustering, "See here, Warfield. I fail to see how this concerns you. The boy is no relative of yours."

"No, but Lady Raincliffe is. She is my cousin and I feel some obligation to keep her out of mischief. A most thankless task." Max lowered his voice, putting an edge of steel into his words. "In fact, sir, you may find me interfering with her a great deal from now on."

General Fortescue's thick gray brows drew together in bewilderment, but Freddie clearly took Max's meaning, for she blushed. Max knew a sense of relief. So the seduction plans thus far were all on Freddie's side and her flirtation with the general had not yet proceeded onto dangerous ground.

Fortescue had no chance to demand any explanation of Max's remark, for at that moment Dora rose dramatically to her feet.

"Well, I for one cannot bear to sit here and see that p-poor boy dragged off to his doom." With a mighty sob she buried her face in her handkerchief and rushed out of the room.

"Now see what you have done." Fortescue glowered at Max. "You have greatly distressed Miss Applegate, and her such a solid, sensible sort of gel. B'gad if there was not a lady present, I would deal you a leveler." Still spluttering his indignation, Fortescue spun on his heel and went charging after Dora.

Left alone with Freddie, Max shifted uneasily. He knew she was every bit as upset as Dora, but he did not think she would render him uncomfortable with a bout of weeping. Far more likely, Freddie would pursue the general's suggestion and attempt to hit him.

Max could have dealt with either response. But he was not prepared for the pleading way she looked at him, fixing him with those wide blue eyes.

"Max, if you could just try to understand about Jack," she began.

"I understand quite well what mischief a boy can get up to. I once enjoyed any number of scrapes myself."

"All the more reason you should sympathize with Jack. Do you know why he ran away? He's been abandoned at that school. He never leaves there, not even to go home."

"That is a great pity, but—"

"He is a younger son, Max, considered of no importance by his father. Jack is so spirited, so lively, the image of his grandpapa. I daresay Sir Wilfred despises him for that. Leon and Wilfred were ever at odds with each other."

A younger son, of no importance. The words caused Max to wince inwardly, like Freddie had raked sharp nails over old memories, clawing at hurts Max had long glossed over. He sighed.

"I could say I do understand, even sympathize. But that doesn't change things, Freddie. Jack is Sir Wilfred's son. You cannot think that you could keep him here forever."

"No, all I am asking for is just a little longer. The child never had a proper holiday. That is why he took such an absurd risk, running away. He wanted to see the sights of London. If you could allow me one more day to take him around—"

"That would be madness, Frederica. I am trying to avoid having you caught with the boy in your company."

"I would be very discreet."

The notion of Freddie being discreet was enough to make Max snort aloud. But before she could press her argument further, Jack appeared at the door of the parlor.

He was scrubbed clean, his hair brushed, his stocky frame garbed in a fresh jacket. Yet he still presented a forlorn figure with his small bundle of possessions clutched in his fists. He avoided acknowledging Max, his gaze directed wistfully at Freddie.

"I am r-ready to go back, Grandmama." Jack blinked fiercely.

Max knew well the effort that took, striving at all costs to avoid babyish tears, to be a man when one was not quite.

When was the last time he had allowed rein to feelings of misery, permitted himself an unmasculine display? Oddly enough, it had been only two years ago when word had reached him of his father's death. He had sat, his brother's letter gripped in his hand, a hot tear escaping down his cheek as he had grieved for the loss of an affection that never had been.

As Freddie moved to wrap one arm around Jack, Max turned away from the pair of them. He hardly knew what had happened to himself this past week. He had cultivated such a hard shell during his years of exile. Cast off by his family, he had formed the selfish determination to remain aloof, never burden himself with anyone else's cares. It was bad enough that he was already embroiled in the chaos that was Freddie. He was not about to be drawn into young Jack's woes.

And yet, as though from some great distance, he heard himself snap, "Oh, very well, Frederica. I will take the boy back day after tomorrow. You may have your excursion with him around London.

"But—" he added sternly before she and Jack grew too boisterous in their rejoicing, "I am going with you."

The next morning it took Freddie more than a few tries to adjust the ribbon strings on her bonnet. She seemed to have more thumbs than fingers, and the strange flutterings she experienced beneath her rib cage did nothing to help. Although delighted by Max's capitulation, she had a good many qualms about him accompanying her and Jack.

The talk she had had yesterday in the park with Max had been wonderful, lifting aside a veil of ancient misunderstandings. But she did not fool herself into thinking that the years would suddenly melt, that she and Max could slip back into the same easy camaraderie they had known when he had been her childhood hero. For one thing, she was obliged to admit he had changed.

She saw little trace of the reckless youth who had once been so marvelous about entertaining a hoydenish little girl. The years had cast Max into a mold of adult stiffness. He no longer seemed to know how to unbend to children.

As Freddie scooped up her shawl, she could not help recalling Max's gruff reactions of the day before. He had been on the point of leaving when she had displayed to him Till's darling baby. Max had kept a wary distance, his only remark, "Does it bite?"

Even being assured that the babe had as yet cut no teeth did nothing to dispel his unease. But many men were uncomfortable around babies. It should be much easier for Max to deal with a lad of ten.

But Jack, for obvious reasons, had taken a dislike to Max. He not only saw him as the enemy, but, Freddie feared, in some strange way her courtly young gallant perceived Max as a rival as well.

Thus it was with some trepidation that Freddie joined the two gentlemen where they awaited her in the parlor. She had prolonged her dressing, hoping they might get to know each other better in her absence. If nothing else, they could join together in bemoaning the dilatoriness of females. But as Freddie crossed the threshold, her heart sank. Jack and Max stood at opposite ends of the room as stiff and stubborn as the pillar supports holding up the roof.

Max consulted his watch, his attitude one of impatience, a decided let's-get-this-blasted-thing-over-with. Although outwardly polite, Jack's bright eyes clearly conveyed the message, we-would-do-just-as-well-without-you-sir.

Gritting her teeth, Freddie maintained a manner of determined cheerfulness and shepherded both of them out of the house. Max's carriage stood waiting at the curb. It would have been a great help if Max had brought his high perch phaeton, such a delight to Jack's boyish soul.

Instead, Max had chosen a more sedate traveling gig that caused Jack to growl under his breath. "Humph. Fit for nothing but old ladies to go racketing about the park on Sunday."

He did brighten a little to see a spirited chestnut hitched in the traces. Jack scrambled up onto the seat of the vehicle himself while Max offered Freddie his hand.

"May I take a turn at the ribbons?" Jack asked eagerly.

"Certainly not," Max snapped. He assumed his own seat and gathered up the reins, giving the nod to the groom to stand away from the horse's head.

With an expert flick of Max's wrist, the chestnut started down the cobblestone street with a jaunty step.

Wedged between Max and Freddie on the narrow seat, Jack heaved a disappointed sigh, which made Freddie long to remind Max that he had once let a little girl much younger than Jack hold the reins of his precious horses. But as Max eased the carriage into the flow of London traffic, his countenance was so dark and forbidding, Freddie kept silent.

The three of them would keep company together only this one day. Freddie supposed they would all survive it. She did not know why it seemed desperately important to her that Jack and Max learn to like each other, that this outing be a shining success.

Perhaps it was because that on the morrow Jack had to leave and Freddie knew she would never be permitted to see him again. She had grown fond of the young scamp for his own sake as much for the fact that he was Leon's grandson and reminded her so poignantly of her lost friend. And perhaps it was because in some odd way she felt she was about to lose Max as well.

A temporary truce existed between them because of Jack's holiday. But Freddie had no doubts as to what would happen when Jack left. She remembered Max's terse warning that after Jack was back in school, Max would return to "deal with her." He fully intended to interfere with her own plans to remain independent, likely still wanted to foist her off onto the charity of his sisters.

Freddie brought herself up short, attempting to cast out such gloomy thoughts. This was no time for her to lapse into a fit of the blue devils and ruin Jack's holiday. Max's surly humor was bad enough.

She slipped her arm around Jack's shoulders. The

boy continued to stare with disgruntled longing at the prancing chestnut.

"Cliveden never lets me drive either," Jack grumbled.

"Cliveden?" Max asked with a frown.

"His eldest brother," Freddie filled in.

"Aye." Jack's chest swelled with indignation. "He thinks he's top of the trees simply because he's going to be a viscount someday. He says I don't need to learn to handle a team 'cause I will be naught but a country parson joggin' about on an old mare."

"Does he indeed?" Max's jaw clenched. He might already have begun to be irritated by Jack's chatter, but somehow Freddie did not think so, for a moment later Max added with gruff but genuine interest, "And what do you say about that?"

"Not a great deal." Jack propped his chin on his hands, his expression gloomy. "Cliveden is always far too ready to carry tales back to Papa or my tutors. The time I put the raspberry jam in his beaver hat only earned me extra Latin lessons. And as for milling him down, I tried that, too. Clive only shoved me away and thrashed me with his riding crop. He is nearly seventeen, so much taller than me."

"He won't always be. Someday when he comes thrusting his nose into your affairs, you'll be able to draw his cork." Max spoke these words with such grim satisfaction, Freddie wondered at what point he must have punched his own elder brother in the nose. Max added, "From the size of your shoulders, you're likely to grow up to be quite a bruiser."

"Do you truly think so?" Jack asked anxiously.

At Max's staunch affirmative, the boy's eyes lit up. Max's words must have conjured up an agreeable vision of the future for Jack, for he stretched back, a beatific smile lighting his features. The tension between him and Max eased just a little.

By the time they reached their destination and Max escorted them into the vast arena of Astley's Amphitheatre, Jack was bubbling over with as much excitement as any ten-year-old. Lustily Jack cheered the pony races, calling particular encouragement to one little dappled gray until he was hoarse. Some of her own anxiety eased, Freddie was able to gasp along with Jack in amazement at the skill of a conjurer and laugh at the antics of the clowns.

If Max was bored, he gave no sign of it, regarding both Freddie and Jack with a kind of avuncular amusement. He placed a hand on Jack's shoulder, gently easing him back in his seat when the eager boy leaned too far over the partition, showing every sign of being about to land headfirst in the ring.

Although Jack had been delighted with the ponies, he was absolutely enthralled by the grace and agility of the acrobats. His ambition to be a Bow Street Runner quite forgotten, Jack cried, "Now, that is what I should like to do when I am grown. That would be something dashing."

Freddie and Max exchanged a smile over the boy's head, though Max's was a trifle wistful. "Poor little chap," he murmured. "He may as well dream while he can. They'll likely have him stuffed into a clerical collar before he knows where he's about."

"Never. Not Jack," Freddie whispered.

"The army or the navy, then. Or he'll be obliged to marry an heiress. Younger sons must be gotten rid of somehow." Max pulled a wry face. "I've often thought if the eldest and heir is healthy, the rest might as well be drowned at birth like a parcel of unwanted pups."

"I would never favor such a practice. I am decidedly fond of younger sons." Freddie tipped her chin to a challenging angle, her gaze locking with Max's. For once his expression was not sheltered beneath those hooded lids. He stared straight back at her, a glow akin to gratitude in his eyes, gratitude and something more. A warmth stole in her heart and at the same time caused her to shiver, tingling with awareness of that powerful masculine presence.

She realized that Max had not changed with the years nearly so much as herself. She had grown from a child to a woman, and Max's nearness, the appreciation simmering in his steel gray eyes, made her glad of it. When she had made the offer to be his mistress, she had done so mainly to torment him. Now she could not help thinking that it was too bad that he had refused.

Freddie blushed hotly, shocked at her own wayward thoughts. She quickly looked away, reminding herself why she was there. She was, after all, a grandmama on an outing with her grandson.

Yet when they exited the amphitheatre and Max tucked her arm within his own, she made no effort to pull away from him. The protective gesture seemed so right, so familiar. Perhaps for one afternoon, she, too, could take a holiday from her fierce pride and lean a little on Max, reveling in the aura of strength, of pure male possessiveness that emanated from his lean, hard frame.

While the groom brought Max's carriage around after the performance, Jack practiced a few handsprings until he was red-faced and panting with exertion. Max growled at Jack to settle some of his wild spirits before he spooked the horse. As ever high strung, the chestnut was pawing in the traces, impatiently tossing its mane, resisting the groom's efforts to calm it. Jack crept toward the horse's head himself.

"Jack!" Freddie protested, starting forward to drag the child back from those restless equine feet, those flashes of large teeth, Jack's small hands seeming in danger of being snapped from his wrists.

But to her astonishment, Max stayed her, watching intently as Jack stroked the horse's velvety muzzle, murmuring soothing words. The chestnut quieted all at once, as though some sorcerer's wand had been waved above its head.

The groom stepped back respectfully, remarking to Max. "Young master's got the way about him with the beastie, eh, sir?"

"Yes," Max said slowly. "Yes, indeed he has." The light in his gray eyes grew almost hazy, like the mists that rolled over London in the early morning. He seemed to be lost in the memories of some far distant time, perhaps of the boy he himself once had been. It jolted Freddie to realize how much in tune she was with his feelings, what he was thinking. She knew what he was going to do before Jack did, perhaps even before Max did himself.

When they were all once more settled into the carriage, Max thrust the reins at Jack, saying abruptly, "Here."

"Sir?" Jack stared at the leather looped in his hands, his breath caught between wild hope and bewilderment.

Max settled back, regarding him with a lazy lift of his brows. "You did request to drive, did you not?"

"A-aye, sir, but you said—"

"Are you going to argue or commence? You should not keep the horse standing about."

"No, sir!" His eyes huge in his round face, Jack turned earnestly to his task. But he was quivering with so much suppressed excitement, he slapped the reins too hard, nearly causing the chestnut to bolt.

Max's strong arms came around the boy immediately, his much larger hands covering Jack's smaller ones. Murmuring words of advice and encouragement, he guided Jack to a lighter touch.

Absurdly Freddie found herself obliged to look away, hide a sudden smarting of tears behind her eyes. If she lived to be a hundred, she thought she would never forget that moment. Long after this day was lost to her, she would remember the look on Jack's face when Max placed the reins in his hands.

But most especially she would remember Max, the deep rumble of laughter from his chest, the light that shone from his eyes as he shared in the boy's delight.

Max balanced Jack's sleeping form in his arms, carrying the boy up the stairs to the second floor landing of Freddie's town house. She preceded him up the darkened stair, the single taper in her hand lighting the way.

The soft glow of the candle spilled over Jack's cherubic features, his mouth still sticky from the lemon ice he had recently enjoyed, his lips curved with some secret dreamings, perhaps of taming the lions and tigers he had seen in the Royal Menagerie.

The boy had had a full day of it, treats from Gunther's famous pastry cook establishment, a drive down Pall Mall, where Jack was rewarded by a glimpse of the prince emerging from Carlton House, a leisurely tour of London's infamous Tower, whose most dangerous prisoners these days seemed to be the collection of wild animals in the yard. Certainly not the brief outing Max had intended upon first setting out that morning. But he had to admit he had only himself to blame. It had been he who had kept thinking up excuses to prolong the excursion, strangely loathe to allow this day to end. Only when Jack's weary head had dropped upon Freddie's shoulder had Max finally given up and headed his horses for home.

Even at the door he could have surrendered the care of the boy to Freddie's butler. But his excuse had been the boy's weight would be too heavy for the nearsighted old man. He had visions of Stubbins walking with Jack into the rail, both of them tumbling headlong down the steps.

But in truth Max liked the way the child nestled so trustingly in his arms, stirring tender sensations Max had never thought to possess. Recovering from his youthful infatuation with his brother's bride, Max had long ago resolved not to marry, burden himself with the care of a wife and babes. That at least was one advantage to being the younger son. He was under no obligation to produce an heir.

Yet, as he gazed down upon Jack, he was consumed by a sudden longing, a bleak feeling that there might be something in life he had missed.

A rather idiotic notion to be coming from one who considered himself a confirmed bachelor. Max gave himself a brisk mental shake. Likely he also had had too long a day and was suffering from a surfeit of lemon ices and tigers, a little boy with an engaging grin and a vagabond lady whose blue eyes could have melted a heart of stone.

Max followed Freddie to the small bedchamber at the end of the hall. He eased Jack down onto the bed, but quickly, and stepped back as though already seeking the distance he had found so comfortable. Freddie lit the oil lamp, the burning wick casting a rosy glow over the room.

She began to strip Jack out of his garments, the boy roused only enough to regard her muzzily through the entire process. Max had an impulse to help, but he quelled it. In any case, Freddie stood in no need of aid from him. Crooning soothing words low in her throat, she eased Jack into a nightshirt many sizes too large for him, smoothing the fabric over his small frame with those comforting gestures only women seemed to know how to make. Watching her with the boy stirred a curious ache in Max's chest.

Feeling very much in the way, he backed across the threshold, mumbling something about waiting for Freddie in the hall below. Absorbed in tucking up the child, Freddie nodded. She was on the verge of extinguishing the lamp when Jack's eyes fluttered open again. "Grandmama?"

Freddie rustled back to his side in an instant. "Yes, love?"

"I had a bang-up holiday," the child murmured sleepily.

"I am glad to hear it."

"You must tell Mr. Warfield that I said thank you and—and I am sorry I did not like him so much at first. You see, I thought you were going to have him replace my grandpapa."

Freddie smiled, caressing the boy's cheek. "No one would ever be able to replace your grandpapa, dearest."

Why were those soft words like a knife thrust to Max's heart? His presence just beyond the door undetected, Max felt like an intruder. Yet he did not seem able to tear himself away from the sight of Freddie bending over the child like some spritely guardian angel, her golden curls tumbling about a face that was as dreamy-eyed with innocence as the boy's own.

She snatched up the reticule she had been carrying earlier and began fishing within its silken depths. "I have something I have been saving to give to you, Jack. Now seems as good a time as any."

At the prospect of a gift, like any eager child Jack came more fully awake, sitting up in bed. From where he stood, Max could see Freddie press something into the child's hands, a small gilt-framed miniature.

Jack stared at it with wide-eyed wonder. "Why, 'tis a portrait of me. However did you manage to obtain my likeness so quickly?"

"Not you, my dear. 'Tis your grandpapa when he was about your age. It was one of the few portraits left to me after he—he went away and I had to leave Dunhaven." She ducked her head, continuing in muffled tones. "There is a more recent portrait of your grandfather, a quite magnificent one that used to hang in the front hall. I believe your papa has moved it to the gallery at the back at the house. If . . . when you ever go to visit Dunhaven, you might just want to have a look at it."

"So I shall." Jack clutched the miniature as though it were a treasure, his small chin stiffening with resolve. "And if I ever can manage it, I shall move that picture back to the main hall, where it belongs."

"That . . . that would be good. I am sure your grandpapa would have been very proud of you, very pleased."

Jack tipped his head to peer beneath the cascade of hair shielding Freddie's face. "Faith, lady, you are not going to cry on a fellow, are you?"

Freddie shook her head, trying to smile. "No, 'tis only I shall rather miss you, young Master Jack."

And she enveloped the boy in a fierce hug. Fearing that he had already witnessed more than he had any right, Max turned and beat a quiet retreat.

As he neared the darkness at the top of the stairs, he paused.

He could hear Dora's voice below calling out something to the ancient Stubbins and the old man's cheerful reply. Then came the definite cooing sound of a babe and distant echoes of feminine laughter, both Dora's and that little housemaid's. It was odd how sound carried in Freddie's house. Perhaps it was the lack of furniture.

More likely it was the warmth that seemed to pervade this half-mad, topsy-turvy household so different from the precision and the quiet he insisted upon in his own.

Max rubbed his fingers against his eyelids, thinking perhaps it might be best not to wait for Freddie after all. He could as easily speak to her in the morning when he came to fetch the boy. He would be better rested then, better able to deal with that brand of delicious madness which ever seemed to follow in her wake.

But Max formed this resolve a trifle too late. Before he set one foot on the stair, Freddie slipped out of Jack's room, squinting toward the shadows where he stood.

"Max?" She breathed. "Is that you?" She stepped forward, holding the wax taper aloft with a soft laugh. "You should have taken the candle away with you or you will be bumping into the walls like my poor Stubbins."

She glided forward, bringing light to his darkness, candleshine picking out the golden glints in her hair, the jewellike facets of her eyes. Max felt an almost irresistible tug of attraction and drew back stiffly.

"So did you manage to coax Master Jack to sleep?" he asked.

"No, but he soon will be. He is quite exhausted."

"The boy needs his rest. I fear I must come early to fetch him away. You look rather done in yourself, so I had best bid you good night."

Max stepped down the first two risers, but Freddie darted forward to intercept him, placing one smooth, cool hand over his on top of the post.

"I never got the chance to thank you," she said.

Being slightly below her brought her face closer to a level with his. There was no escaping the sweet, earnest expression in her eyes, the slightly shy smile. It was obvious Freddie's own defenses were down tonight which made this situation doubly dangerous.

Max eased his hand from beneath hers. "Thank me?" he said. "For what?"

"For your kindness to a small boy today. And also to another child many years ago."

"No thanks are necessary. It was a very careless sort of kindness, my dear. I never do anything that proves an inconvenience to me."

"Don't you? I suppose that is why you insist upon driving Jack yourself all the way back to school. You could send him on the stage with a servant to accompany him."

"It so happens I have an inclination myself to travel in that direction."

"Oh, I am sure. During the height of the London season, most gentlemen experience this urge to go haring off to the wilds of Yorkshire."

She was laughing at him, but Max found he did not mind that nearly as much as he pretended. "Minx," he growled.

Freddie blushed as prettily as though he had just paid her a compliment. But her saucy look faded, an anxious furrow appearing between her brows.

"Jack will be all right, won't he, Max? You don't think his tutors will—will beat him or anything?"

"Not if they place any value on their heads," Max said grimly.

"And what about Sir Wilfred?"

"Oh, I think I can handle him as well. I have a good many scores to settle with that gentleman." His resolve to keep his distance already forgotten, Max could not resist running his fingertips over the tiny creases of her brow.

"I know you don't have much cause to believe in my promises, Freddie. But I assure you that I will do all in my power for Jack, to see him bestowed safe and sound."

Her eyes shone with such gratitude, it took his breath away. A gratitude he felt far from deserving. Before he could stop her, she caught his hand and pressed a gentle kiss against the back of it. Max snatched his hand away as though he had been stung. Her lips had felt so soft, so delicate. For all her bravado, it was borne in upon him how vulnerable she really was. And how helpless he was to protect her.

"Damme!" he said. "If I could only tuck you safely back into the schoolroom as well."

She wagged her brows at him in teasing fashion. "Alas, sir, I fear I am a bit old to be sent back to stitching samplers."

He was worried nigh to distraction, and *she* was making jests about it. "I am quite aware of your age, madam. You are not so easily disposed of as young Jack."

"Disposed of?" she echoed. He thought a flash of hurt appeared in those speaking blue eyes, but she rallied behind a quick smile. "Yes, like Jack, I always have been something of a nuisance to my relatives."

"Curse it all, Freddie! You know I did not mean—"

"But," she said brightly, "I am no one's problem now."

No one's but her own, Max thought with a frown. The outing with Jack had distracted him from the immediate threat to his peace of mind, Freddie and her blasted list of eligible rakes, whatever outrageous plans she might be forming.

She attempted to brush past him, precede him down the stairs. But he caught her arm, detaining her on the landing. "When I get back from Yorkshire, Freddie, I want you ready to close up this house and move to Lady Bentley's. Then we will sit down and discuss what is to be done with you."

"That might not be convenient. I will likely be out with General Fortescue."

"Freddie! I want an end to this nonsense. You will never form any sort of connection with Fortescue. You are only trying to provoke me. I know you are not the sort of woman to engage in such a liaison."

"Alas, I fear you are quite mistaken. If you want a true notion of my character, you have only to ask Aunt Jameson or Sir Wilfred. Don't go about telling everyone, but . . ." She leaned forward and said in a conspiratorial whisper, "I am a very wicked woman, Max."

Max was not even tempted to smile. "Ever since you were a little girl, you have gotten up to your naughty tricks, thumbing your nose at the world's disapproval. But you are too old for these childish games of defiance now. This reckless way you have been living . . . gaming, flirting, talking about becoming someone's mistress—it is a little more dangerous than climbing trees or purposefully blotting your copybook. You are going to get hurt, Freddie. And what is more, you are going to hurt the people who care about you, believe in you."

"And who might that be?" she asked softly. She looked up at him, her eyes lit up with a wistfulness that rivaled the candle's glow.

"There is Miss Applegate for one."

"Dora completely understands and approves of everything I do."

"And then there is young Jack."

"He is going away."

"And—and your household. Stubbins and that little housemaid."

"And what about you, Max?"

He shot her a look of pure exasperation. "Damn it, of course I care what happens to you, you little fool. Why else would I be trying to make arrangements for you, place you somewhere safe, where I don't have to worry about you anymore?"

Her face fell. She said tautly, "Well I *certainly* would not want to worry you. But I refuse to be dependent upon anyone's charity. Not even yours, Max."

"You would rather trade yourself to some old man for a few trinkets?"

She flinched a little at his bluntness, but replied steadily enough. "Yes, I fear that I would. Besides, it would not be as crude as you describe it."

"How would you know? How many times have you been anyone's mistress before?"

Freddie's face settled into that expression of mulelike stubbornness that Max had ever found so exasperating. "None," she admitted. "But I have learned and observed a great deal since coming to London."

"You have learned nothing. You are green as any chit out of the schoolroom. Someone ought to show you exactly what it would be like to satisfy the demands of a wealthy lover."

"Perhaps General Fortescue will oblige." The

candle wavered in Freddie's hand. She kept her chin upraised in defiance, but she felt wearied, unequal to continuing this quarrel with Max. She wished he would simply go away, but he continued to block her path to the stairs.

He seemed calm enough, but a hard, dangerous light had sprung to his eyes, which she found very unsettling. He groped inside his waistcoat pocket, drawing forth several golden guineas which he counted out into his hand.

"Wh-what are you doing?" she asked.

"Nothing." His smile was grim with determination and not particularly pleasant. "I have merely come to the conclusion that if anyone shows you anything, it should be me. After all, you did ask me first."

"Ask you what?"

"If I wanted you as my mistress."

"B-but you said no and I was only teasing you when—" She retreated an involuntary step as Max stalked closer. "Oh, don't, Max. I am too tired for any more lectures or you trying to teach me a lesson."

"No lesson, my dear," he murmured, his voice both silk and steel. "Merely a simple business transaction."

He took her left hand, upended her palm, pressing the guineas into it, forcing her fingers to curl about the coin. "There. That should take care of a new bonnet or a gown. Now, what will you offer me in return?"

"A box on the ears!"

"Wrong." Max pressed closer. She was forced back another step. "That is not the correct response, Freddie. That is not at all what a lover who paid handsomely for your favors would expect."

He backed her all the way against the wall, so that she nearly stumbled over the hall table.

"Stop it, Max," she cried, her heart thudding with a strange mixture of fear and excitement. She tried to hand the money back to him. But he snatched the candle from her instead.

His eyes holding hers with an intensity and heat that left her breathless, he blew the candle out, leaving them in darkness. He set the taper down upon the hall table and reached for her. The coin tumbled from her fingers, jangling across the floor. Freddie attempted to bolt. But Max yanked her hard against him.

She struggled wildly, but he pinned her hands with ease. His mouth found hers, taking her lips in a hard, plundering kiss, sending a jolt through her entire frame. She stiffened. Unable to defy his strength, she sought to make herself icy, unyielding, until he should pull back in defeat.

But he surprised her by gentling the kiss, his mouth now whispering softly over hers. His bullying she could resist, but his tenderness proved her undoing.

Against her will she found herself relaxing against him. No! She knew why he was doing this. It was only Max trying to frighten her, to demonstrate to her what a naive fool she was. She would not give in to the delicious warmth that had begun to steal over her.

But his lips worked magic in the darkness, teasing the corners of her mouth, caressing her cheeks, tasting the curve of her jaw. A soft sigh escaped her as he released her wrists, his arms circling protectively around her.

He murmured her name as he kissed her once more, and suddenly Freddie no longer cared why he was doing this. She melted against him, returning his kiss, awkwardly at first, then with increasing eagerness.

He coaxed her lips apart. Slowly, seductively, his tongue invaded the moist recesses of her mouth. She gasped at the shock of such intimate contact, then found the sensation almost unbearably sweet. She was hazily conscious of how well she fit against Max's hard-muscled form, of how right it felt to be in his arms.

All thoughts of resistance gone, she buried her fingers in his hair, giving herself up completely to his embrace. She did not demur, even when Max's kiss became even more demanding, his hands moving over her feverishly, stroking an ache of longing within her, feelings of desire that should have terrified her but did not.

When his mouth moved down to caress the pulse pounding at her throat, she arched her neck back with a soft whimper of pleasure. Max drew back a little, breathing raggedly. He did not release her, but she sensed him fighting to regain control.

"Freddie, this is madness," Max groaned. "What am I doing?"

"Perhaps," she whispered, "perhaps you do want me after all."

Her words had a strange effect on him. He wrenched her arms from his neck and put her away from him. He took a step back. Even in the darkness Freddie could see how unsteady his hand was as he raked it back through his hair.

She longed to be able to clearly see his face. She longed to know if he was feeling the same powerful currents as she. More than anything, she longed to be back in his arms.

But then he spoke, saying the words she most dreaded to hear.

"Freddie, I am sorry." And the regret in his voice

told her all she needed to know. She had taken a tentative step toward him, but she stopped, left suddenly chilled, bereft.

"I never meant to . . . that is, I had no right—" he stumbled on. "Damn! I have behaved like a perfect boor."

She wanted to beg him to stop. The last thing she desired was for him to apologize for what had been some of the most wondrous moments of her life. But she could not seem to speak past the thickness gathering in her throat.

He sighed. "I fear this lesson got a little out of hand."

A lesson . . . that was all the past few moments had been to him. How stupid she had been to lose sight of that fact.

"Don't fret, Max," she managed to say hoarsely. "It was not entirely your fault. I have always been entirely too precocious."

He gave a shaky laugh. "Kissing like that was not exactly what I was trying to teach you. I think I had best be going. Doubtless we are both just overtired."

Was that how he kissed when he was exhausted? She could not help wondering with a tiny shiver what Max was like when he was well rested. Not that it mattered. She had a sinking feeling she was never going to be permitted within a yard of Max Warfield again. He was already moving toward the stairs.

She felt as though she could not bear to let him go like this.

"Max!" she cried desperately.

He had descended the first riser, but she sensed him pause, shifting to glance back at her.

"Max, I . . ."

"Yes?" His tone was not encouraging.

Freddie was suddenly glad of the concealing shadows. She groped through the darkness, seeking her abandoned pride until she found it.

"Nothing," she said. "I wanted only to bid you good night."

"Good night. I will be back in the morning for the boy. See that Jack is ready." Max started quickly down the stairs. Shortly thereafter, she heard the front door closing behind him.

Freddie touched one hand to her lips, still tender and tingling from the force of Max's embrace. Part of her wished she had made more of an effort to detain him, and part of her was glad he had left and so quickly, too.

That was all that had saved her from making a complete idiot of herself. One moment more and she might have been tempted to tell him just how much she wanted him.

Another moment longer and she might have confessed how much she needed him. And one more moment and she might have done something really foolhardy.

She might have told him that she had fallen in love with him.

Chapter 10

Freddie had not dreamed of Leon once since his death. But during the many days following Max's departure with Jack into Yorkshire, Freddie's slumberings were frequently disturbed by a vision of her late husband.

Leon appeared to her just as he had been on their wedding day, garbed in his elegant brocades and lace-trimmed cravat, his silvery hair tied back in a queue. He stood waiting outside the church, a stately presence beaming reassurance. And she was a nervous bride again, clad in that awful pea green silk Aunt Jameson had bestowed upon her most grudgingly for a wedding gift. Freddie stumbled on her own train and Leon caught her, easing her tensions with one of his dry jests, saying that while he hoped one day she might come to fall in love with him, he had never meant for her to do it so precipitously.

The scene was all so clear that Freddie was nigh driven to cry out in her sleep. Only when Leon escorted her into the interior of the church did the vision begin to seem more dreamlike. She could see naught of the pews, only shifting mists and glowing candles. She clung tighter to Leon simply to find her way down the aisle.

But to her dismay, he tugged his hand free. "Nay, my dear," he said. " 'Tis time to let go."

She looked up at him uncomprehendingly. He gave one of those gruff laughs that crinkled the lines around his eyes. Shoving her gently on her way, he urged, "Go on now, sweeting. Would you be late for your own wedding?"

Freddie took a few faltering steps forward, then glanced back toward Leon. But he had already faded into the mists. She had no choice but to creep forward, groping to find her way.

Suddenly the altar itself loomed up before her and another figure stood waiting. Tall, strong, and steady, the waves of night dark hair swept back from his brow. Familiar hooded eyes watched her, not with their usual brooding cynicism, but lit by a smile of great tenderness.

"M-Max?" Freddie murmured.

He held wide his arms. A sob of joy escaped her and she started running forward. Running, but no matter how she tried, she seemed unable to reach him. The church floor spun out from beneath her and she was falling, tumbling down into the relentless white mist.

It was at that point she awoke to discover the morning sun streaming through her bedchamber window. She was not fighting the mist but her own bedcovers. She sat up slowly, hugging her pillow to her chest.

"Damme!" she said, drawing in a shuddering breath. Three times! Three times since she had last seen Max she had had that nightmare or one very like it. If she believed in portents the way Dora did, she might be tempted to think that Leon was in some way attempting to communicate with her, to tell her something. Perhaps even . . . to give her his blessing?

Freddie murmured, "If that is the case, you are quite off the mark, old friend. There is nothing to bless."

How could one give a blessing to a wedding when the bridegroom was so unattainable, vanishing into the mist? She sighed, trying to shake off the feeling of hopelessness, telling herself it had been only a ridiculous dream after all. But like many dreams, it had a disturbing way of mirroring the waking world.

For Max was indeed out of her reach. He had not needed a fog to accomplish his disappearance, either. Yorkshire had done just as well. Freddie had the miserable feeling that Max could not flee from her far or fast enough.

If she had any doubts on that score, she had only to think back to that morning when Max had come to fetch Jack away. She had spent a dreadful night after that scene on the stairway landing, tossing and turning, hoping that when she awoke, this strange madness would have passed like a brief but virulent bout of influenza. But it hadn't. As soon as she had seen Max again, she had felt the longing to fling herself into his arms. The sight of him was at once familiar and strange, as though she had always known this man, known she would come to love him one day, as though she were seeing him for the very first time, the feelings coursing through her startling and new.

But Max had, as always, been Max, cool, with the customary briskness in his manner, her very distant cousin. In the hubbub of bidding Jack good-bye, soothing Dora's sobbing, trying not to cry herself, Freddie had not even found time for a private word with Max.

No mention was made of what had passed between them the night before. Max bundled Jack into his traveling carriage and Freddie thought he meant to depart without another word. But at the last second he had paused, regarding her with a frown.

"You will be all right while I am gone?" he murmured.

"Of course," she had said cheerfully. She could hardly tell him she did not think she was ever going to be all right again.

"I suppose it would be pointless to ask you to promise not to do anything rash in my absence."

Freddie had hesitated but an instant, then replied softly, "Yes, I promise."

But Max was already following Jack into the coach and Freddie was not sure that he had heard her. Blinking back her tears, she had stood waving until the carriage vanished down the street, watching Max go with a mixture of love and resentment.

Foolish man! She would have promised him anything he asked, and he had not even noticed.

If he gave her any thought at all during his sojourn in Yorkshire, Freddie knew what it would be. Stow Freddie someplace where she could no longer be a nuisance, where she would no longer cause Max a moment's worry. At one time, she had mightily resented that attitude.

Of late she was feeling dispirited enough to oblige him. True to her promise, she had done nothing more to forward her plan of finding herself a wealthy protector.

Max had been odiously correct. She was a naive little fool, quite incapable of carrying off such a clandestine arrangement with the aplomb of Lady Deidre McCauley. Especially not now, realizing how she felt about Max. Even if Max would never be aware of her love, never return it, to offer herself to any other man seemed to Freddie the worst sort of betrayal.

Which, she thought glumly, brought her right back to where she had started, trying to find some other way to survive. She had discovered during the past few days that Max had directed his man of business to pay off most of her debts. Loving him as she did, Freddie found the prospect of accepting his charity more intolerable than ever. Going begging back to Aunt Jameson was equally unthinkable.

Lady Bentley had once offered Freddie the use of that house in Bath. Max's pressure upon his sister notwithstanding, Caroline would still be quite eager to see the last of Freddie.

Freddie could not avoid the melancholy conclusion that Lady Bentley's suggestion offered Freddie her only real choice. She could live more cheaply in Bath. In order to salvage some of her pride, perhaps she could offer to act as caretaker of the place, obtain positions for Till, Stubbins, and Dora as well. Freddie had a shrewd notion Lady Bentley would agree to anything simply to get Freddie out of London.

The prospect of spending the rest of her life in Bath was not the most appealing one. But what did that matter? Far better to put distance between herself and the city, herself and Max. Confirmed bachelor he might be, but there was still the unfinished matter of that wager at White's. Someone would win it eventually. A man like Max was not meant to be celibate. He would be bound to take a new mistress, perhaps Lady Channing. Freddie wanted to be far away when that happened, where she would catch no hint of the rumors, no glimpse of Max driving the lively brunette through the park in his phaeton, waltzing with her at a ball, slipping off to some balcony, kissing her as he had Freddie, not to teach any lessons, but with wholehearted passion.

Even imagining Max with another woman in his arms was enough to drive Freddie half mad with jealousy. She doubled her pillow over her head in an effort to blot out the unwelcome images.

It was thus that Dora found her when the older woman whisked cheerily into Freddie's bedchamber, bringing her a steaming cup of chocolate.

"Are you awake, Freddie?" Dora cried in a jolly, booming voice. " 'Tis past ten. This is most unlike you to—"

She pulled up short, regarding Freddie's position with some perplexity. "Have you got a headache, my dear? I don't think using that pillow as a compress will serve the purpose. It would be far better to let me bathe your forehead with Hungary water."

Freddie shifted the pillow from her head, feeling singularly foolish. "You know I loathe Hungary water, Dora. Besides, there is nothing wrong with my head. I . . . I was just testing out a new remedy for—for straightening unruly curls."

"Indeed?" Dora asked with great interest, and Freddie winced with shame at her own falsehood, wondering how long it would be before she found Dora with a pillow strapped to her own head.

She sought to divert Dora's attention by accepting the saucer and cup, thanking her friend for her kindness although at the moment Freddie had no appetite for anything, let alone the sticky sweet chocolate.

She forced herself to sip it while Dora plunked down on the edge of her bed. It was often Dora's habit to visit upon rising, settling in for what she termed a comfortable prose. Freddie had never felt less like sharing confidences. She replied to Dora's nonstop chatter in monosyllables, trying to make her responses fall at the appropriate times.

Despite her own cloud of distraction, Freddie could not help observing that something was different about Dora this morning. She scrutinized her friend closely for a moment, then realized what it was.

"Dora!" She interrupted her friend in mid-sentence. "You cut your hair."

"What? Oh, that. Yes, I did." Dora patted her short bob of curls with a self-conscious gesture. "Or, rather, Till did. She is very skilled at such things."

"It is quite fashionable and most becoming," Freddie said, and that was not merely a kind lie. The style was more suitable to Dora, the cluster of ringlets softening the angles of her face.

Dora blushed at the compliment, the color enhancing an unexpected brightness in her soft brown eyes.

"Your complexion has improved, too," Freddie continued. "At least the air of London seems to agree with one of us. You make me feel positively haggard by comparison."

"You have been looking a little pale of late, my dear." Dora reached out to give Freddie's hand a motherly pat. "But I daresay you will be feeling much better when Mr. Warfield returns from Yorkshire."

"Why would you suppose that?" Freddie asked with some dismay. Were her feelings for Max that mortifyingly obvious?

Dora beamed at her. " 'Tis only that I have observed that you seem in much finer fettle when Mr. Warfield is about, even when you are quarreling with him." She paused to vent a sentimental sigh.

"The two of you looked so charming that day you took Jack out for his holiday, just like a little family. Mr. Warfield was astonishingly attentive. I almost wondered . . ."

Dora shot Freddie a nervous sidelong glance. "Now, don't be angry with me, dear. But I almost wondered if Mr. Warfield might be thinking of marriage?"

Freddie pulled a wry face. "Far from it. In fact, the night before he left, he reconsidered my offer to be his mistress."

Dora looked a little crestfallen, then rallied. "Of course, that must have pleased you. That *was* what you wanted."

"No, I was only pretending when I made Max that offer."

"Oh, dear. How very awkward it must have been when he decided to take you up on it."

"No, he was only pretending as well."

Dora's brow puckered, then she shook her head. "Being a wicked woman can be very confusing sometimes."

"Yes, it can," Freddie agreed gloomily. She did not feel equal to broaching the subject of the future with Dora just then. But she owed it to her friend to tell Dora as soon as possible of the decision she had reached.

Freddie set the cup of barely tasted chocolate on the bedside commode and straightened. "Dora, I have been doing a great deal of thinking. Bath is really not such a dreadful place. It might even be amusing to go there and take the waters. Perhaps we ought to take Lady Bentley's advice and—"

"And leave London?" Dora cried.

Freddie had not been certain exactly what Dora's reaction would be, a little disappointment perhaps, but nothing like the stricken expression that crept into her friend's eyes.

"Oh, no, Freddie. You cannot mean it. You would not want to leave London now." Dora cast down her eyes, coloring deeply. "Not just when—when everything is becoming so interesting."

"A little too interesting for me," Freddie said dryly. She entertained a fleeting memory of Max's kiss and was hard pressed not to blush herself. "I could use a little quiet."

She forced herself to meet her friend's gaze frankly. "The truth is, Dora, I no longer know what else to do."

"But what of your plan to find an eligible rake?"

"I fear I am no more successful at that than I was at cards."

Dora bit down upon her lower lip, then said hesitantly. "There is always General Fortescue. He calls practically every day, stays for tea. Perhaps if you ever joined us . . ."

"The general is a kind man, but we are simply not well suited. As I told you days ago, I have quite given up on my plan to attach him."

"So you said. But, oh, Freddie, are you quite certain?" Dora asked, staring at her with a peculiar intensity.

"Very certain," Freddie said firmly.

"But he has applied for tickets to the museum at Montagu House and is coming around later this morning to escort us there and to the circulating library."

Museums? Libraries? Neither of these sounded much like the rakish old general, but Freddie felt too wearied to give the proposed expedition much consideration.

"I am sure it would be most diverting, Dora," she said. "But I fear I must beg off."

"The general will be disappointed."

"Then you accompany him."

"Oh, dear, I am not sure that I should. I feel so wicked to always be taking your place."

"My dear Dora, I have no claim upon the man," Freddie said impatiently. "You have my full permission to go off with the general, flirt with him, and be as wicked as you like."

Freddie shifted lower on the bed, nestling her head back onto the pillow. She had not had a headache when Dora entered, but she felt the nigglings of one now.

Dora rose to her feet. She emitted a tremulous sigh. "If you truly mean that . . ."

"I do!" Freddie said, wishing Dora would stop hemming and hawing, simply leave her in peace. She rolled over to her side. "Now, pray, you must excuse me. I find I am still very tired. I have not been sleeping too well of late."

"And here I have been chattering away at you." Dora was instantly contrite. "I should let you get your rest. You have been worrying too much again about how we shall get on and with never any help from me."

"Nonsense," Freddie murmured. "You have always been a great support to me."

As Dora hovered, Freddie grimaced, fearing her friend would now stay, fussing over her. But Dora did no more than lay her hand upon Freddie's brow, her touch gentle and soothing.

"Go back to sleep, dear," she cooed. "And don't you fret about moving to Bath or any other such. I will take care of the general and . . . and everything."

Freddie had a hazy notion that perhaps she ought to ask what *everything* was. But her headache was already escalating into a full throb. She closed her eyes, scarcely aware when Dora slipped out of the room.

Max approached the steps of Freddie's town house with some trepidation. The quickening in his veins was no doubt owing to the fact that he never knew what might be taking place behind Freddie's walls, what fresh disaster awaited, what latest chaos lurked, threatening to pull him in like a whirlpool.

In all honesty, Max had to admit it was not entirely such apprehensions that sent him scurrying to her doorstep only an hour after his return. Upon arriving back in the city, he had but paused long enough at his own house to change his traveling clothes.

As he strode up to her door, this eagerness, this peculiar unsettled feeling, was new to him. But he had finally arrived at some conclusions regarding his emotions and Freddie, hard-won conclusions after many distracted days during his sojourn in the north.

He had scarce been able to get Freddie off his mind for a moment, vexing, tantalizing sprite that she was. Never had there been any woman who could make him lose his temper so swiftly, who could so easily overset his self-control. He had always been a man to let his head rule even in his amorous relationships with women.

And then came Freddie.

He should have known something was different that night on the staircase landing when he pulled her into his arms to teach her a lesson. The lesson had been his to learn, one of passion and tenderness, desire and a deeper longing than he had ever experienced before.

He had wanted to spend eternity with her heart

pounding against his. He had wanted to hold her protectively, fiercely, in his embrace forever. And he had wanted beyond all thought, all reason, to make love to her there and then. Her shy but eager response to his kiss had been nearly enough to overset any scruples he had. And also enough to rouse his suspicions regarding the exact nature of Freddie's relationship with her late husband. She was astonishingly innocent for the widow of as old and accomplished a rakehell as Raincliffe.

He did not know why that should relieve him so. It was ridiculous this continuing jealousy of his over the part that the viscount had played in Freddie's life. Perhaps it was owing to his fear that Freddie yet mourned too much for her beloved Leon. Max had devised a new plan for Freddie's future, and was more than a little afraid that she would reject it.

Unaccustomed to such nervous qualms, irritated by them, Max seized the door knocker and rapped it with more force than necessary. He rocked back on his heels, trying to curb his impatience, knowing that it took Stubbins forever to answer the door.

He was therefore almost thrown off balance when the door was flung open. It was not the half-blind butler who blinked up at him, but Freddie herself.

She looked quite breathless, her golden hair a wild tangle, as though she had just arisen from her bed. This conjured up a far too agreeable image for Max, and he fought to quell his quick arousal. Harder to quell was the desire to gather her into his arms. God, how he had missed her these past two weeks.

She stared almost blankly at him, then stumbled back, saying, "Oh, Max. It's only you."

Max winced. He never knew what sort of reception he was going to get from Freddie. Only one thing was certain. She never failed to disconcert him.

"Thank you," he said, crossing the threshold and closing the door behind him. "It's good to see you again, too."

"I didn't mean ... 'Tis only that I thought—I hoped you might be Dora."

Max removed his high-crowned beaver and began stripping off his gloves. He tossed them on the hall table. "Never tell me you have managed to mislay Miss Applegate."

He was astonished when his wry jest elicited no answering retort. He glanced up, for the first time noticing how pale Freddie was, the deep circles rimming her eyes.

He immediately crossed to her side, taking her hand. "Freddie? What is it, my dear?"

Freddie swallowed hard, too close to tears to be able to speak.

"Is it something to do with Miss Applegate? Good heavens, the woman cannot truly be lost?"

Freddie shook her head.

"Do you fear there has been some sort of accident?"

Another negative.

"Then what the deuce is amiss?"

Freddie drew in a deep breath, then blurted out, "Dora—sh-she has run off with General Fortescue."

With all the will in the world Max could not seem to help himself. A bark of incredulous laughter escaped him.

Freddie glared at him. "This is not amusing."

"No, I am sure it would not be," Max said soothingly. "If it were true. But Dora and Fortescue? I fear you have been letting your imagination get the better of you."

"*This* is not imagination." Freddie took an object

she had been clutching in her other hand and thrust it at him.

Max accepted it, staring at the crumpled piece of vellum. He raised an inquiring brow.

"It's a letter from Dora," Freddie said. "Delivered just before you arrived. Stubbins accepted it, so I had no chance to question the messenger. You just read that and then see if you are inclined to laugh."

Frowning, Max obeyed, smoothing out the sheet of paper. Miss Applegate possessed a fine, neat hand. It was a pity, Max thought as he scanned the page, that she did not also possess a clarity of expression.

My dear Freddie,

I must write you in haste, for the general is all afire to be gone. He did not obtain tickets for the museum after all because his mother lives in Hampstead. Forgive me for my wickedness, but I will not be home for tea. The general has begged so ardently, what could I do but say yes and so I am off with him in a coach and four. Well, it is more of traveling brougham, actually, but don't worry, for I will send you my address directly. Do not serve up those raspberry tarts in the pantry for I fear they have gone bad.

Most affectionately yours,
Dora Margaret Applegate

As he reached the end of this missive, Max placed a hand to his brow, his head throbbing with the effort to make sense of Dora's letter. He supposed he could read it again, but he doubted that it would do much good.

He refolded the peculiar message while Freddie

paced the length of the hall, fretting. "It is all my fault."

"What is? You mean about the raspberry tarts?"

"No! Dora and Fortescue. It all becomes so clear now."

"Then I wish you would explain it to me," Max said irritably. "I thought Fortescue was dangling after you."

"He was, but after I promised you that I would stay out of trouble, I stopped seeing him. But he still kept coming around to tea. If I had not been so selfish, lying about moping, I might have noticed what was going on. All this time he has been plotting to seduce my poor Dora."

"Forgive me, Freddie. Your friend Miss Applegate is a very fine woman, but she is scarcely the sort to invite seduction. She is a little too—er—*solid* for such a thing."

"She *was* before she came to live with me. But I told her it was all right. I told her to go off and be just as wicked as she chose, and now she has."

Max rubbed his neck and vented a weary sigh. He was exhausted from his recent journey, and this was not at all the sort of tête-à-tête he had hoped to enjoy with Freddie. Despite the jumbled letter, he still had trouble accepting the notion of Dora Applegate being wicked with anybody, even an old devil like Fortescue. But Freddie clearly believed her friend's virtue to be in imminent peril. Max sensed how distraught she was, only her fierce pride preventing her from dissolving into tears.

She turned to face Max, proclaiming dramatically. "If anything happens to Dora, I will never forgive myself. I have been the most deplorable influence on her. Go ahead and say it, Max. You warned me I was courting disaster and I would not listen."

"There will be time enough later for me to say I told you so. Right now I suppose we had best do something about recovering Miss Applegate."

Freddie bit down on her trembling lip. "When I answered the door just now, I hoped that it was her, that perhaps Dora had come to her senses and returned."

Max thought that anyone who could write such a muddle-headed letter very likely had no senses to come back to. But he wisely kept such a reflection to himself. Instead, he asked, "How long has Miss Applegate been missing?"

"She went off late this morning on an outing with the general." Freddie stomped her foot, her eyes glittering with sudden anger. "That old villain! I might have known he never had any tickets to the museum."

Max let this confusing statement pass. He consulted his pocket watch. " 'Tis nearly five o'clock. If she did go off somewhere with Fortescue, which, mind you, I still cannot quite believe, the most they could have is a few hours' start."

"I shall have to hire a carriage and try to follow them."

"Don't be ridiculous," Max said. He reached for his hat and gloves, already bowing to the inevitable. "I will go in search of her."

"That is very good of you, Max," Freddie said. "But Dora is my friend. I see no reason why you should be bothered."

"Don't you?" Max said. "Let us just say that I suppose I had better grow accustomed to dealing with these unusual situations."

Freddie looked confused by this cryptic comment, but Max was not about to go into any explanations just now.

"My first step," he said, "will be to make inquiries at the general's lodgings."

Freddie looked as though she might be inclined to give him an argument. But finally she said, "Fine. If you insist upon it, I suppose I would be grateful for your help. Just give me a moment to fetch my shawl and bonnet."

"Freddie, I think it would be better if you waited here."

"I'll do no such thing. It will be far too humiliating for Dora to have you come upon her alone. She will need me."

"And what about Fortescue? If he does have improper designs on Miss Applegate, he will be less than pleased by my interference. There could be a most unpleasant scene."

"All the more reason I should be there," Freddie retorted. "To keep you from doing anything rash. This is the sort of situation that frequently involves gentlemen in some ridiculous duel."

"Yes, by God, I suppose it is," Max said, a slight smile curving his lips.

"Now what the devil amuses you?" Freddie snapped.

"Nothing," Max said dryly. "Only that I have never fought a duel over a woman in my life. Yet this is the second time this month I may come close to trading blows. And all for the honor of Miss Dora Applegate!"

Chapter 11

Freddie clenched her hands in her lap, leaning forward on the seat of Max's curricle. She peered through the gathering darkness, willing the chestnut to go faster along the road leading out of London. Ominous-looking clouds had gathered on the horizon, threatening to steal away what remained of the daylight.

A rumble of thunder caused her to shrink instinctively closer to Max.

"Perfect," he muttered. "It's going to rain."

"Perhaps the storm will hold off until we reach Hampstead," Freddie said hopefully.

"If we reach Hampstead and don't end up in a ditch first." Max swore under his breath as he guided his curricle past a particularly nasty rut in the road. It was getting increasingly harder to see. He would need to stop and light the running lamps soon.

Freddie sensed the tension in him, the barely restrained impatience. She knew Max believed that they were off on some harebrained chase. Freddie feared much the same thing herself. When they had inquired at Fortescue's lodgings, they could get no answers from the general's tight-lipped valet. But the boot boy had told them he had heard the general planning to set out for Hampstead and with a lady in his company. Yet the shrewd-faced little rascal had demanded a half crown for this information and Freddie was not certain how reliable the lad might be.

She could not help voicing some of her own doubts aloud. "It makes no sense. Dora's letter said something about Fortescue's mother. Why would a man take a woman he had designs upon to Hampstead if his mama was living there?"

"Why would a man take anyone to Hampstead?" Max groused. He tightened his grip on the reins, concentrating on the road ahead. He looked less than pleased with the situation he found himself in, and Freddie could hardly blame him. She knew he had just arrived back from Yorkshire and must be close to exhaustion.

She almost wished it had been anyone else but Max who had arrived on her doorstep, only to find her caught up in a fresh disaster. As if he did not already think her enough of a nuisance, a perpetual scapegrace!

Yet despite the scowl marring his handsome features, Freddie found herself glad of his steady presence at her side. No matter how gruff he pretended to be, no matter how he complained, Max always helped. If anyone could find her poor Dora, Freddie was confident it was he. Max had always fixed everything from her broken dolls to keeping her out of debtor's prison.

There was only one thing past his power to mend, her breaking heart. Having him so close, having to hide the fact she loved him was the most indescribable torment. She longed to press a kiss against the hard set of his lips and had to scoot a little farther away on the seat to suppress the temptation.

As the curricle rattled onward, Freddie thought anything might be better than this grim silence that had settled over them. She sought to break it by inquiring after Jack. That seemed a safe enough topic.

"Was all well with Jack when you left him? It has been so hard thinking of him back at that horrid school."

"But he isn't," Max said. "He's been moved to Eton, where I went as a lad. My old master, Dr. Douglass, is still there. If he survived dealing with me, he can do the same with Jack. He'll look after the boy, see that he gets sent home for holidays. Jack will even be permitted to receive any chance visitors that happen his way."

"Oh, Max. You don't mean that I could . . ."

At Max's nod, Freddie exclaimed, "However did you persuade Wilfred to agree to all of this? He is such an insufferable bully."

"Only where women and children are concerned. But I fear I am something of a bully myself, besides possessing the advantage of taking regular sparring exercises at Gentleman Jackson's."

"You never hit Wilfred?" Freddie asked, torn between horror and delight at the notion.

"How does one hit a man cowering behind a settee?"

For the first time since Max had gone away, Freddie felt an inclination to laugh.

Max continued. "My clinching argument with Sir Wilfred was more in the nature of blackmail. He has great ambitions for the unprepossessing Cliveden, hopes he will cut quite a dash in the world. I informed my lord if he did not pay more heed to his younger son, Cliveden will not be cutting anything, anywhere. Especially not in the London clubs like Brook's, White's, anyplace where I hold influence."

"Max," Freddie said admiringly. "You are utterly ruthless."

"Yes, I am when it concerns getting my own way." He shot her a sidewise glance and looked about to say something more.

But at that instant a jagged streak of lightning cut the sky, illumining the distant shapes of the houses of Hampstead. Though often described as a village on the fringes of London, it was more the size of a small resort town these days, noted for its spring water.

As Max's chestnut labored, drawing the curricle up the hill, Freddie wondered with some despair how they would ever go about searching for Dora. The streets with its close-packed rows of cottages and lodgings was nigh as bad as London.

"What do we do now?" she murmured, trying to curb her mounting fear that it might already be too late to save Dora from being compromised. "We can hardly go about knocking at every door."

"Our best chance is to inquire at the inns," Max said. He risked a glance upward at the uncertain sky. "If nothing else, we will be near shelter when the storm breaks."

Freddie offered no disagreement as he sought out the nearest inn. It was a snug stone structure whose creaking sign proclaimed it to be the Good King Harry. It appeared to be neither an establishment of the first order, nor one entirely disreputable.

When Max drove into the yard, an ostler came forward promptly to help with the horse. As Max lifted Freddie down from the curricle, he commanded, "I want you to hurry inside. I already felt a drop. I will be in as soon as I make inquiries of this fellow. Even if Fortescue did not stop by here, it is possible the ostler may have noticed the carriage passing through."

Freddie was reluctant to obey, but the wind was picking up, tugging at her bonnet and shawl. When Max gave her a nudge in the direction of the inn, she went.

Entering the long, narrow taproom, she meant to make some inquiries of her own. But she saw no sign of anyone. Before she could locate the host, Max had joined her. The rain had begun to tap against the windows, and he brushed beads of moisture off his hat and greatcoat.

"The luck appears to be with us," he said with grim satisfaction. "A couple answering very closely to the description of our truants arrived at this inn about an hour ago." He looked around him with distaste. "Though if Fortescue were planning a tryst, one would think he could do better than this."

"This is hardly the time to be criticizing another man's seduction methods," Freddie said. "That fiend may have Dora abovestairs even now."

Her heart pounding with dread, she started toward a rather rickety-looking banister, the creaking wooden steps that led upward to the next floor.

But she had not even mounted the first riser when a woman wearing a soiled apron came through the taproom door from the region of the kitchens. She had a heavy, drooping bosom, an even heavier scowl.

"And where do you think you are going, miss?" she demanded of Freddie. "We have no more accommodations available here."

"We are not seeking a room, my good woman," Max said. "What we desire is—"

"I have a fair idea of what the pair of you desire." The woman looked Max and Freddie up and down, her eyes dark with condemnation. "But you won't find it here. This is a respectable establishment."

Max's brows flew up in his haughtiest expression, but the effect did little good when his hair was so windblown. Freddie touched a hand to her own disordered curls crushed beneath her bonnet. She was suddenly conscious of what a disreputable pair she and Max made.

"Please, ma'am," Freddie said, trying to be placating. "My cousin and I are very tired. We are searching for—"

"Cousin indeed!" The landlady snorted. "Be off with you. I need no more trouble. I already regret letting my private parlor to that other pair. Said he was a general. What kind of general travels with no servants and his lady, not even a nightgown to her name!"

Freddie scarce heard the rest of this diatribe, the only words that registered with her being "private parlor." She glanced around anxiously for another door and saw one to the right of the bar counter. She rushed forward to open it, ignoring the landlady's furious expostulations.

Freddie burst into a small wood-paneled dining chamber. It was bare of furnishing but for an oak table and a few chairs. Fortescue was seated on one of them, Dora pulled down onto his lap, gasping and struggling to be free.

"Unhand her, you villain," Freddie cried, running forward. It was not until she began raining blows upon the startled general's arms and head that she realized that far from being in distress, Dora was breathless with laughter.

Her giggles stilled at the sight of Freddie. She leapt up from Fortescue's knee, her cheeks turning bright pink.

"Freddie!"

Fortescue had flung up one arm to defend himself. He peered cautiously around his sleeve. " 'Pon my word! Lady Raincliffe. What a surprise."

"Not as surprised as you are going to be, you— you miscreant rogue," Freddie spluttered. "I don't know what lies you told Dora to get her to come away with you, but you shall be sorry for it."

"Oh, Freddie, no!" Dora whisked herself in be- tween Freddie and the general.

But Freddie thrust her aside, glowering menac- ingly at Fortescue. Quite forgetting her own resolve to prevent any dire confrontations, she blurted out, "Max Warfield is here, too. If you have offered Dora any insult, he—he will call you out for it."

"He mustn't," Dora wailed. " 'Tis too soon for me to become a widow. I just got married."

"Married!"

The stunned echo did not come from Freddie, but Max. He had finally managed to force his way past the irate landlady. As he crossed the threshold, Freddie was not sure if he looked more amused or ready to strangle someone.

Freddie had a fair idea who that someone might be. She put a hand to her throat and sort of qua- vered. "M-married?"

Fortescue snapped to his feet in his best military manner, looking both sheepish and proud. "That's right, b'gad. We meant to keep it secret awhile longer until I have had a chance to break the news to my mother." He took Dora's hand, beaming down at her. "But you must allow me to present you to the new Lady Mordant Fortescue."

Dora blushed deeply and lowered her eyes. Fred- die was glad Fortescue had vacated his chair. Her own legs no longer seemed able to hold her. She sagged onto the wooden seat, her mind reeling. "Married?" she repeated. "Dora, what does this mean?"

"I explained it all in my letter," Dora said. "The general did not have tickets to the museum. He had a special license instead."

"I am afraid you forgot to mention that," Max drawled.

"Did I? Oh, dear."

"We were married in the little church at the head of the lane," Fortescue said. "M'parents wed there when they eloped. Family tradition, eh what?"

Freddie still felt too stunned to take it all in. Max appeared to have recovered faster. He shook the general's hand with surprising good humor for a man who had just been dragged off on a useless quest to save a lady's virtue.

He was even demanding his right to kiss the bride, when he was interrupted by the sounds of a fracas coming from the taproom.

He grimaced. "The landlady, no doubt. She threatened to return with reinforcements to cast us all out."

When Dora gave a small cry of alarm, he added, "Don't fret. I will deal with our gracious hostess." He moved briskly across the room, intercepting the red-faced landlady just as she was about to burst over the threshold. He forced her back out, closing the door behind him, muffling the sound of the ensuing argument.

Dora bustled over to Freddie. Bending down before her, she caught both of Freddie's hands. "Are you all right, my dear? I did not mean to cause you such distress. I am sorry I did not make my note more clear, but I was so distracted. Mordant's proposal took me so by surprise. But everything will be wonderful, Freddie. You will see. I am a married woman. I finally will be able to repay you for your kindness, rescuing me from a lifetime of only being

Sir Wilfred's poor relation. Now I will be able to take care of you."

"Oh, Dora," Freddie said, eyeing her friend in horror. Regardless of the general's presence, she whispered, "Please do not say that you have sacrificed yourself for me."

"No." Dora gave a tinkling laugh. She cast a fond look up at the general which he returned. "I have been falling in love with this dear, foolish man ever since we met."

"Why didn't you tell me?" Freddie asked.

"You had enough to worry about, and for a long time I thought you were interested in the general." A wistful look came into Dora's brown eyes. "Even after you relinquished all claim, it still seemed so silly, the notion of me being in love, that anyone could love me in return. I never imagined that anything so romantic and daring as an elopement could ever happen to a plain, ordinary spinster."

The general tut-tutted and loudly objected to Dora's description of herself.

Dora gave Freddie's hand a squeeze. "I trust you are not so very angry with me, dear?"

"No, I was only worried. I thought—" But as she gazed down into Dora's honest, open countenance, Freddie broke off with a tremulous smile. "Well, never mind about that."

"I know my behavior has been most irregular," the general said. "But I do hope you will give us your approval, Lady Raincliffe."

"Dora does not need my approval."

"Indeed I do," Dora said. "You are my dearest friend. I should be truly miserable if I thought you could not be happy for me."

Freddie did not reply at once. She angled a fierce glance up at the general. "You truly love her, sir? You promise to take the best of care of her?"

"My word of honor upon it, my lady," Fortescue said gruffly, gradually softening into his rogue's smile. "She is the sort of woman I have always needed to keep me out of trouble, don't you know? Such a solidly sensible sort of gel!"

Freddie turned back to Dora. Her friend hunkered before her, regarding her with huge, pleading eyes.

"So what do you think?" Dora asked anxiously.

"I think," Freddie said, brushing back a stray tendril of Dora's hair, "that you make the most beautiful bride I have ever seen."

Dora emitted a half sob of relief, and she flung her arms around Freddie. They hugged, laughed, cried until the general cleared his throat, looking mighty uncomfortable with this feminine display of emotion.

"I hate to remind you, my dear," he said to Dora. "But we must be going soon."

"Oh! Oh, yes." Dora straightened hastily. When Freddie gave her a puzzled frown, she said, "We stopped here after the ceremony only to have a sort of wedding supper. This is not the sort of place Mordy approves of to spend the night."

"Bad sheets," the general explained. "Too many holes. We plan to travel on to m'mother's estate, just beyond Hampstead."

"And I am so nervous about meeting her," Dora moaned.

"Nonsense. She'll adore you just as I do." The general winked at Freddie. "Mama is also a most sensible sort of a gel."

"Afterward," Dora continued, "we are going to Rome. Imagine me, Dora Applegate traveling abroad."

"Dora Fortescue," Freddie reminded her with a

tender laugh. While the general left to see about the carriage, she helped bundle Dora into her cloak.

Beset by a last-minute attack of nerves, Dora clutched at Freddie's sleeve, murmuring, "I wish you were going with me."

"Goose! On your bride trip?"

"But I feel so guilty. I have been so thoughtless, so inconsiderate. Who is to look after you?"

"I still have Till and Stubbins. Now, stop your fretting."

"When we get back, you are to come live with us. Even Mordy has said so."

Freddie made no reply. There was time enough to argue that point after Dora returned. She was a little anxious about her friend traveling during a storm, but when the general returned to fetch his bride, he assured Freddie the rain had already slackened off to a mere drizzle.

As the general linked his arm through Dora's, she looked so radiant, Freddie felt a lump form in her throat.

Dora sighed. "I am so very happy, Freddie. And I owe it all to you. None of this would have happened to me if we had not come to London to be wicked women."

Freddie laughed. She managed to keep smiling as Dora and Fortescue left the room.

"Good-bye, Freddie," Dora called. "I shall be sure to write. I am going to miss you very much."

It was only after Dora had gone that Freddie murmured, "And I shall miss you, too, my dear friend." She had not realized quite how much until that moment. A strange sensation of melancholy stole over her, and she felt left quite alone, abandoned.

She ought to be nothing but delighted for Dora and she was berating herself for her own selfishness when Max returned. He strode into the parlor, complaining. "Can you credit it? That infernal landlady had actually summoned the constable. I thought we were all going to spend the night in jail, like some wandering brigands. It is astonishing what an outlay of blunt it takes to convince people of one's respectability. But it all comes of hanging about with runaways like—"

Max paused, frowning as he gazed around the empty room. "And where the deuce is the happy couple?"

"Gone," Freddie said. "Fortescue really does have a mother near Hampstead. They are journeying on to her house."

"What!" Max's sharp tone caused her to jump. "You mean that shatterbrained woman has just gone off and left you?"

"This is Dora's wedding night," Freddie reminded him. "I think I would be infinitely de trop."

"Do not either of you possess a single wit? I have done my best to convince that harridan of a landlady of our respectability. And here you are, left alone with me, at night, at a public inn. If this ever gets abroad, your reputation will be in tatters."

"I have never worried overmuch about my reputation."

"I know."

Max shot her an impatient look. "Fortunately, there is a reasonable solution. You will have to marry me."

"What!" Freddie felt all the color drain out of her face.

"Perhaps I did not put that as well as I might." He raked his hand back through his hair with a rueful gesture. "Damn it, Freddie. I keep turning phrases over in my head, but none of them seem quite right. What I mean is . . . would you do me the honor of becoming my wife?"

"No!"

The vehemence of her reply appeared to take him aback, but he recovered, saying dryly, "If you are that uncertain of your answer, don't worry. I will give you more time to think about it."

Freddie faced him, trembling. Why did he not simply thrust a knife through her heart and be done with it? Because she had just witnessed Dora's glowing happiness, this grudging offer from Max was all the more painful by contrast.

"I don't need any more time," she said. "You don't have to do this, Max. I am going away—to Bath."

"What the devil does Bath have to do with my offer of marriage?"

"Because it is a place away from London and— and away from you. I don't know why you have this sense of obligation, this absurd notion that you are saddled with the responsibility of looking after me, even to the point of sacrificing yourself on the altar of matrimony."

"Freddie!" He started toward her, but she backed away, her eyes filling with proud tears.

"I have already had a lifetime of people doing their duty by me, Max," she whispered. "I don't want any more of it, especially not from you."

Spinning on her heel, she rushed blindly out of the parlor. She brushed passed the landlady in the taproom, scarcely registering the woman's disapproving expression. Freddie bolted out the inn door, into the night, the rain misting against her cheeks to mingle with her tears.

She did not know where she was going, and she didn't care, only seeking to escape Max. But she did not get far when he overtook her.

Seizing her by the shoulders, he spun her around. "Freddie! What do you think you are doing? Come back inside before you get soaked and catch pneumonia."

"Leave me alone, Max," she cried, trying to twist away from him.

He swore. "I should have known better than to expect you would make this easy." He seized her shawl and dragged it up, arranging it like a scarf to shield her head from the rain. He did not seem to realize his own hair was already dripping with moisture, plastering to his head.

"You little fool," he murmured. Only Max could turn such words into an endearment. The light spilling through the inn windows illuminated his face. Freddie shrank from the tenderness she saw glowing in his eyes, not daring to place any faith in it.

He held her fast, saying, "Do you really believe I would ask a woman to marry me out of a sense of duty? You obviously have no comprehension of what a selfish man I am."

Freddie sniffed. "I suppose you are going to try to convince me you have been overcome with a sudden passion for me. Like some sort of a fit."

"More like a consumption. It comes over you so gradually, you don't realize you've caught it."

"And just when did this affliction strike you?" Freddie tried to lace her words with scorn, but her voice cracked.

Max stroked back a tendril of her hair which was by now very damp, as bedraggled as she felt. "Oh, the signs were always there if I had but had the wit to interpret them. That night I nearly lost control, kissing you on the stairs. The way I have been driving myself half mad, worrying what to do with you. The simplest solution has always been to find you a new husband. But I never seemed able to get around to considering any candidates. I finally said to myself, Max, you dolt. Why not marry the girl yourself? No, my nobler half argued. You want better for Frederica than that."

His lips quirked into a lopsided smile. "But as usual, my selfish side won out. You will never know all that you have brought back into my life, Freddie. You taught me to care again. So I am asking you most humbly, will you marry me?"

Her lips quivered. "You are being very stupid, Max. Offering marriage to someone as desperate as me, with no prospects. I might just accept you. And then where would we be?"

"Happy, I hope," he said solemnly. "But I don't want you thinking you have to accept me for that reason. You do have other choices. I did not spend all that time in Yorkshire solely on Jack's behalf. I did some investigating into the terms of your late husband's will."

"You wasted your time, Max."

"Regarding the will, perhaps I did. But I uncovered another interesting fact. There is a portion of the Raincliffe estate by tradition that has always been set aside to provide for the viscount's widow. A dower house. Living there would not make you wealthy, but you would remain independent."

"Wilfred would never permit such a thing."

"Oh, I think I could guarantee that he would. So you see, Freddie, you do have a choice. You can go on being Leon's widow, the dowager viscountess. Or you can settle for being plain Mrs. Warfield."

Freddie gazed up at him, stunned, heedless of the rain trickling down her face. "You—you did that for me? When you could easily bully me into marrying you, at the same time, you offer me an escape?"

"Quite magnanimous of me, isn't it?" He reached

down to cup her chin, his fingers firm and warm. "I failed you once, Freddie. I never want to do that again. I—I may never be able to replace Leon—"

"I would not want you to try. Leon was my very dear friend. He will always have a place in my memory. But you, Max"— she swallowed thickly— "I have carried you in my heart for a very long time. I love you. That is why you must be really sure of your reasons for wanting to marry me. I could not bear it if I ever lost you again."

"You won't." He held out his arms to her.

She hesitated but a moment more, then with a mighty sob cast herself into his arms. He kissed her, straining her close, murmuring, "I love you, Freddie. Come in out of the rain."